Prodigal Son

SUSAN MALLERY

SILHOUETTE
SPECIAL EDITION®

First published in Great Britain 2006
Large Print edition 2006
Silhouette Books Limited, Eton House,
18-24 Paradise Road, Richmond, Surrey, TW9 1SR

© Harlequin Books S.A. 2006

Special thanks and acknowledgment are given
to Susan Mallery for her contribution to the
FAMILY BUSINESS miniseries.

ISBN-13: 978 0 373 60371 8
ISBN-10:   0 373 60371 1

Set in Times Roman 17 on 22½ pt.
36-1206-56615

Printed and bound in Great Britain
by Antony Rowe Ltd, Chippenham, Wiltshire

SUSAN MALLERY

makes her home in Southern California, where the eccentricities of a writer are actually considered normal—what a relief! When she's not busy working on her latest novel, she can be found cruising the boutiques in her quest for yet another pair of shoes. Susan would love to claim to be a famous gourmet chef, but she is not. She does, however, do fabulous take-away ordering and always serves said take-away food on lovely china.

Chapter One

Samantha Edwards had never minded the inter-view process, even when she was the one looking for a job. But having seen her prospec-tive boss naked made things just a little tricky.

The good news was Jack Hanson was unlikely to bring up that single night they'd shared. Not only wasn't it relevant to her em-ployment application, it had been nearly ten years ago. She doubted he remembered anything about the event.

Well, not just the one event. Her recollection

was completely clear. There had been three "events" that night, each of them more spectacular than the one before.

"Ms. Edwards? Mr. Hanson will see you now."

Samantha looked up at the sixty-something secretary behind the modern metal-and-glass desk in the foyer in front of Jack's office.

"Thank you," Samantha said as she rose and moved toward the closed door.

She paused to tug on her cropped jacket. Her clothing choices had been deliberately conservative—for her, at least. Flowing black slacks, a cream-and-black checked jacket over a cream silk shirt. It killed her to avoid color, but ten years ago Jack Hanson had been the poster boy for straitlaced conservative types. She was willing to guess that hadn't changed.

Except he hadn't been the least bit conservative in bed.

The wayward thought popped into her head just as she pushed open the door to his office.

She did her best to ignore it as she drew in a deep breath, reminded herself how much she wanted this job and walked confidently toward the man standing behind his desk.

"Hello, Jack," she said, shaking hands with him. "It's been a long time."

"Samantha. Good to see you."

He studied her with a thoroughness that made her breath catch. How much of his steady perusal was about sizing up the candidate and how much was about their past?

She decided two could play at that game and did a little looking of her own.

He was taller than she'd remembered and he still seemed to exude power and confidence. She wanted to say that was a natural attribute for someone born to money, but she had a feeling Jack would have been a winner regardless of his upbringing. He was simply that kind of man.

Time had been kind, but then time had always preferred men to women, she thought humor-ously. Jack's face showed character in addition to chiseled features. She wondered if life ever got boring for the physically perfect. While he had to deal with things like broad shoulders and a smile that would have most of the female population lining up to be seduced, she had unruly red hair that defied taming, a stick-straight body, small breasts and a butt that could only be described as bony. Was that fair?

"Please," he said, motioning to one of the chairs. "Have a seat."

"Thanks."

He did the same, claiming his side of the desk. He looked good there—in charge and powerful. But she happened to know he was new to the job.

"I read about your father's death a couple of months ago," she said. "I'm sorry."

"Thanks." He motioned to the office. "That's why I'm working here. The board asked me to step in and take care of the company for a while."

"I'd wondered," she admitted. "Last I'd heard, you were practicing law."

"It would be my preference," he told her.

"But you did so well at business school." She would know—they'd been competing for the top spot, often by working together. He'd been the detail-intensive, organized half and she'd been the creative member of the team.

"Hated every minute of it," he said. "I realized I preferred the law."

Jack thought about the day he'd told his father he wasn't entering the family business. George Hanson hadn't been able to comprehend that his oldest son wasn't interested in learning how to run a multimillion-dollar company. The older man had been disappointed and furious. It had been the only time Jack hadn't done what was expected of him.

Ironically, today he was exactly where his father had wanted him to be.

But not for long, he reminded himself.

"I guess your father's death changed your plans," Samantha said.

He nodded. "I'm on a three-month leave of absence from my law firm. Until then Hanson Media Group gets my full attention."

"Are you sure you want the Donald Trump act to be temporary?"

"I'm not the tycoon type."

She smiled. "I would say you have potential. Word on the street is you're bringing in a lot of new people."

"That's true. My father hated to hand over control of anything. He was still the head of at least three departments. With a company this big, no one has the time or energy to run them and the rest of the business. I'm looking for the best people possible to join the team."

"I'm flattered."

"It's the truth. You're only here because you're good. I need creative types. It's not my strong suit."

She smiled. "A man who can admit his weaknesses. How unusual."

"Samantha, the only reason I passed marketing was because I was on your team. You carried me through the whole class."

"You tutored me through cost accounting. We're even."

She shifted slightly as she spoke, causing her slacks to briefly hug her slender thighs. The other candidates had been highly skilled with incredible résumés, but unlike Samantha, they'd come in dressed in business suits, looking equally comfortable in a board room or law office.

Not Samantha. Despite the conservative colors, she was anything but ordinary. Maybe it was the bright green parrot pin on her lapel or the dangling earrings that hung nearly to her shoulders. Or maybe it was that her long, fiery red hair seemed to have a will and a life of its own.

She was not a conservative businessperson.

She was avant-garde and wildly creative. There was an independence about her he admired.

"You left New York," he said. "Why?"

"I wanted to make a change. I'd been working there since graduation."

He studied her as she spoke, looking for nuances. There were plenty, but none of them worried him. Per his research, she was coming off a divorce. Her previous employer had done his best to keep her from leaving.

"You have to know this is a dream job," she said. "You're offering complete creative control of Internet development, with more than a million-dollar budget. How could anyone resist that? It's my idea of heaven."

"Good. It's my idea of hell."

She smiled. Her full mouth curved and he felt himself responding. Subtle tension filled his body.

"You always did hate a blank page," she said, her smile widening to a grin.

"You always did hate rules," he told her.

"Me?" She raised her eyebrows. "You were happy enough to break them when it suited your purpose."

He shrugged. "Whatever it takes to get what I want. What I want now is a great staff and the company running smoothly. Let's get down to specifics."

He passed her information on several current Internet campaigns. After she'd flipped through the material, they discussed possible directions for growth.

Samantha became more animated as the conversation progressed. "Children," she told him. "There's so much we could do for kids. After-school programs on the Web. Not just the usual help with homework, but interactive programs linking kids all over the country."

As she spoke, she leaned toward him, gesturing with her hands to make her point. "We can also cosponsor events with popular movies or TV shows."

"Cross-advertising," he said.

"Yes. The potential is huge. And that's just younger kids. I have even more ideas for teens."

"They're the ones with the disposable income and the time to spend it," he said. When she raised her eyebrows in surprise, he added, "I've been doing my research."

"Apparently. It's true. With more single-parent families and more families with both parents working, teens are often a real source of information on what items to purchase. They actually influence adults' decisions on everything from breakfast cereal to cars. Plus they're computer savvy, which means they're comfortable downloading information. To them, the Internet is as much a part of their lives as phones were for us."

"So you're interested in the job," he said.

"I distinctly recall the word *heaven* coming up

in the conversation. I wasn't kidding. I'd love the chance to grow this part of the company."

Her excitement was tangible energy in the office. He liked that. She'd always thrown herself into whatever it was she was doing and he doubted that had changed.

He'd been surprised to see her name on the short list of candidates, but pleasantly so. He and Samantha had worked well together at grad school. They'd been a good team. Just as important, she was someone he could trust.

"The job is yours, if you want it," he told her. "The formal offer would come from my human-resources person in the morning."

Her green eyes widened. "Seriously?"

"Why are you shocked? You're talented, qualified and someone I'm comfortable working with."

"You make me sound like a rescue dog."

He grinned. "If I could find one that could work a computer…"

She laughed. "Okay, yes. I'm interested. But I have to warn you, I'm very much the creative type. I'll want control of my staff."

"Agreed."

"We're not going to be wearing three-piece suits."

"I don't care if you wear frog costumes, as long as you do the job."

She didn't look convinced. "This isn't like the law, Jack. You can't always find an answer in a book."

"Can I get disapproving and difficult before you give me the lecture?" he asked, mildly amused by her concern. "I get it—creative people are different. Not a problem."

"Okay. Point taken."

She rose. He stood as well. In heels she was only a couple of inches shorter than him. He walked around the table and held out his hand.

"Leave your number with Mrs. Wycliff.

You'll be hearing from my HR office first thing in the morning."

She placed her palm against his. As he had when they'd touched a few minutes ago, he felt a slight sizzle, followed by a definite sensation of warmth somewhere south of his belt.

Ten years after the fact and Samantha Edwards still had the ability to drop him to his knees. Sexually speaking. Not that he would act on the information or let her know how she got to him. They were going to work together, nothing more.

He released her hand and walked her to the door. "How soon can you start?" he asked.

"The first part of next week," she said.

"Good. I hold a staff meeting every Tuesday morning. I look forward to seeing you there."

She hesitated before opening the door. "I'm excited about this opportunity, Jack. I want to make a difference."

"I'm sure you will."

She looked into his eyes. "I wasn't sure you'd consider me. Because of our past."

He pretended not to know what she was talking about. He wanted to make her say it. "Why would knowing you in business school make a difference?"

"Not that."

He waited.

Color flared on her cheeks, but she continued to hold his gaze. "Because of what happened that night. When we…" She cleared her throat. "You know. Were intimate."

"Water under the bridge," he said easily, mostly because it was true. He'd never been one to dwell on the past. Not even on a night that had made him believe in miracles. Probably because in the bright light of day, he'd learned that dreams were for fools and miracles didn't really happen.

Promptly at four in the afternoon, Mrs. Wycliff knocked on Jack's office door.

"Come in," he said as he saved the work on his computer, then looked up at his father's former assistant.

"Here are the daily reports," she said, placing several folders on his desk.

"Thank you."

He frowned as he looked at the thick stack that would make up his evening reading. In theory, he knew plenty about running a company. He had the MBA to prove it. But theory and reality often had little in common and this was one of those times. If one of the employees was accused of homicide—that he could handle. Right now, a charge of first-degree murder seemed simple when compared with the day-to-day ups and downs of a publicly traded corporation.

"How is the staff holding up?" he asked the older woman. Although he was confident Mrs. Wycliff hadn't been born into her position, he couldn't remember a time when she hadn't worked for his father.

She clutched the back of the chair and shook her head in refusal when he invited her to take a seat.

"They miss him, of course. Your father was well liked in the company. Of course he would be. He was a good man."

Jack was careful to keep his expression neutral. George Hanson had been a man of business. He had lived and breathed his company, while his children had grown up on the fringes of his life. That wasn't Jack's definition of *good*.

"Several people have stopped by to tell me how much they miss him," Jack told her. It happened at least once a day and he never knew what to say in return.

She smiled. "We all appreciate you stepping in to run things. Hanson Media Group has been home to a lot of us for a long time. We'd hate to see anything happen to the company."

"Happen?" He'd only been on board a couple of weeks. From what he'd been able to find out, the only problems seemed to be his father's need to micromanage departments. Once Jack got the right people in place, he figured the firm would run smoothly.

Mrs. Wycliff smoothed her already perfect gray hair and absently fingered the bun at the back of her neck. "Your father was very proud of you. Did you know that?"

Jack wasn't fooled by the obvious change in subject, but he figured he would do a little digging on his own before he grilled his assistant for information.

"Thank you for telling me," he said.

She smiled. "He often talked about how well you were doing at your law firm. Of course he'd wanted you to come to work for the family business, but if the law made you happy, he was happy, too."

Jack tried to reconcile that description with the angry conversations he'd frequently shared with his father. George Hanson had tried everything from bribes to threatening to cut Jack out of the will if he didn't come work for the company.

He'd long suspected his father had shown one side of his personality to the world and kept the other side more private.

"We had a deal," he said. "After law school, I got my MBA. Then I decided which I liked better." He shrugged. "It wasn't much of a choice."

"You followed your heart and your talents," Mrs. Wycliff told him. "That's what your father always said." She smiled. "He brought in champagne the day you made partner."

"Junior partner," Jack corrected absently. Champagne? When he couldn't get hold of his father, he'd left a message with Helen, his stepmother, telling her about the promotion. She'd sent a card and a stylish new briefcase as a gift. Ever polite, Helen had signed both their names, but Jack had known it was all really from her. His father had never bothered to call him back.

"He was a good man," Mrs. Wycliff said. "Whatever happens, you have to remember that."

"That's the second time you've been cryptic," he told her. "Want to tell me why?"

She had dark blue eyes and the kind of bone structure that spoke of great beauty in her youth. If she had been a different kind of woman, he would have suspected something between her and his father. But while George might have been interested, Jack was confident Mrs. Wycliff herself would not have approved.

"I can't," she said, her voice low.

"Can't or won't?"

She clutched the back of the chair more firmly and met his direct gaze. "I don't know anything. If I did, I would tell you. You have my complete loyalty."

"But there's something?"

She hesitated. "A feeling. I'm sorry. I can't be more specific. There's nothing more to say."

He'd known the woman all of two weeks, yet

he would have bet she wasn't lying. She didn't know. Or she was a damn fine actress.

Feelings. As a rule, he didn't trust emotion, but gut responses were different. He'd changed his line of questioning during a trial more than once based on a feeling and each time he'd been right.

"If you learn anything," he began.

"I'll tell you. I've been talking to people. Listening." She swallowed. "I lost my husband a few years ago. We never had children and a lot of our friends have retired and moved south. This company is all I have. I'll do anything to protect it."

"Thank you."

She nodded and left.

Mysteries he didn't want or need. As for Mrs. Wycliff, while he appreciated her concern and her willingness to provide him with information, who was to say if they had similar goals? She wanted Hanson Media Group to go on forever, he wanted out. If those two objectives came into conflict, he had a feeling his once-loyal secretary would become a bitter enemy.

With employment came paperwork, Samantha thought two days later as she sat in an empty office and filled out her formal job application, along with pages for insurance, a security pass, a parking space and emergency contact information.

She worked quickly, still unable to believe she'd landed her dream job with little or no effort on her part. She'd been so excited to get going, she'd come in before her start date to do the paperwork.

"Thank you, Helen," she murmured, knowing her friend had somehow managed to get her name on the short list of candidates. She'd wanted to mention that to Jack during their interview, but on Helen's advice had kept quiet. For reasons that made no sense to Samantha,

Jack, along with his siblings, thought Helen was little more than a trophy wife.

Hope I'm around when they all discover that there's a very functioning brain behind those big eyes, Samantha thought.

She signed the application and moved on to the next piece of paper.

"Morning."

She looked up and saw Jack in the doorway to the small office. He looked tall, sexy and just-out-of-the-shower tempting. What was it about a freshly shaved man that got her body to pay attention?

"Hi," she said.

"I heard you were here taking care of details." He leaned against the door frame. "Thanks for accepting the job."

"I'm the grateful one," she said with a laugh. "I can't wait to get started. But first there's all this to work through." She patted the papers. "I've been promised that if I do everything correctly, I get my own ID badge at the end of the day. And the key to my office."

"I heard that rumor, too. My intrepid assistant informed me we already have a meeting scheduled."

"Monday afternoon," she said. "I'll be working all weekend, bringing myself up to speed. I'll want to discuss parameters with you before I set my team on the task."

"You're not expected to work 24-7," he said.

"I know, but I'm excited and it's not as if I have a lot of things planned. I've just moved to Chicago. I'm still finding my way around."

"All the more reason to get out and explore."

She tilted her head. "Hmm, is my new boss *discouraging* me from working? That's a new one."

"I don't want you to burn out your first week. I need you around longer than that."

She knew they were just joking around, and she enjoyed that she and Jack seemed to have kept some remnant of their friendship intact. But why did she have to be so aware of him?

Even now, with him standing several feet away, she would swear she could hear him breathing. Heat seemed to radiate from his body, in a way designed to make her melt.

It had been like this before, she thought glumly. Back in grad school, she'd spent two years in a constant state of sexual arousal. She'd needed the friendship more than she'd wanted a lover, so she'd ignored the physical attraction between them. She'd been careful to always seem disinterested.

Until that one night when she'd been unable to stand it a second longer.

"I promise to explore often and well," she said. "But later. Right now I want to get to work."

He held up both hands. "Okay. I give up. Be a slave to your job. I'll stop complaining." He dropped his hands to his sides. "Are you already settled in your new place?"

"I have exactly two suitcases in my hotel room. It didn't take long to settle."

"Aren't you going to get an apartment?"

"Eventually. I'm too busy to look around right now." A partial truth. Apartment hunting would give her too much time to think. She wanted to avoid bursts of introspection whenever possible.

"My building has executive rentals," he said. "They come fully furnished and are rented by the month. That's how I found the place. I took a two-month lease, found I liked the building and bought something larger."

"Sounds interesting," she said cautiously.

He grinned. "Don't worry. It's a huge high-rise. We'd never run into each other."

Did he think she thought that was a problem? Okay, yeah, maybe it was. She had a feeling that running into Jack outside of work could be a complication, if not outright dangerous for her mental health. But hadn't she promised herself to face life head on? Wasn't she done with hiding from the truth?

"I appreciate the information," she said. "Do you have a phone number or person to contact?"

"I have a business card in my office. Let me go get it."

He walked down the hallway. Samantha turned her attention back to the paperwork in front of her, but instead of seeing it, she saw the empty apartment she'd left in New York only three weeks before.

She'd thought she would always live in New York. She'd thought she knew what to expect from her life. Funny how a lifetime of dreams could be packed up into a half-dozen boxes and the man she'd once trusted to love her forever had turned out to be nothing more than a lying thief.

Chapter Two

"We're working on the, ah, upgrades right now," Arnie said as he shifted in his seat. "The, ah, first set should be, ah, ready by the end of the month."

Jack had to consciously keep himself from squirming in sympathy. In his law practice his clients were usually so distracted by the charges brought against them that they didn't have the energy to be nervous and in court he didn't care if his cross-examination upset a hostile witness.

But Arnie wasn't a client or a hostile witness. He was a techno-geek from the information technology department, or IT, and he was obviously uncomfortable meeting with his new boss.

Jack glanced down at the report in front of him, then back at Arnie. "Sounds like you're totally on schedule," he said, then smiled at the other man. "Good for you."

Arnie swallowed. "Thanks. We've been trying. Roger, my, ah, boss, sort of said we had to. Oh, but not in a bad way."

"I appreciate your effort," Jack said, wishing Roger, Arnie's boss, had been available for the meeting. Jack couldn't take much more of the poor man's suffering.

"You're going to be working with Samantha Edwards," Jack said. "She started today. She's very creative and energetic. I'm sure you'll be impressed by her ideas."

And her, Jack thought, wondering what Arnie would think of Samantha's tall, slender beauty and infectious smile. Or maybe he didn't have to wonder. Harsh, but true, Arnie looked like the kind of guy who never got the girl. He was pale, with thinning brown hair, light brown eyes and glasses. He wore a plaid short-sleeved shirt and jeans, and his posture yelled, "Please don't hurt me."

Arnie's face contorted as if he were trying to decide if he should smile or not. "I heard there was going to be a lot of Internet expansion. That's good for my department."

"It will be plenty of work," Jack told him.

"We can do it. I'm sure of it."

"I am, too," Jack said. "Once Samantha finalizes her plans, she'll get with you and your guys to work out the details. We may have some capacity issues. I don't know enough about the technicalities to know. I need you to stay on top of that. And help coordinate the launch date. We need to be aggressive, while being realistic."

Arnie nodded vigorously. "Okay. Sure. I can do all that. But, um, you know, George was never interested in the Internet. He always liked the magazine side of the business."

One of the reasons the company was in big trouble, Jack thought. Magazines were expensive propositions when compared with the relatively low cost of maintaining a Web site.

"I see Internet expansion as a quick and cost-effective way to build the business. After the initial start-up costs, we're spending much less." He frowned. Shouldn't an IT guy know this?

"Oh, I agree," Arnie said quickly. "I think it's great. So do most of the guys in my department. But, you know, not everyone will agree."

Jack didn't like the sound of that. "Like who?"

Arnie instantly looked trapped. "Oh, it's—"

"We're a team here," Jack said. "We're only as strong as our weakest member." Hopefully that would be the hokiest thing he had to say this week, he thought grimly. But if it worked…

Arnie squirmed some more, ducked his head,

sighed, then said, "Roger, my boss. He's not real big on change."

"Interesting," Jack said, wondering how someone like that rose to the level of running the IT department. Or maybe Jack's father had wanted it that way, considering his disinterest in all things high tech. "I appreciate you telling me that. I won't mention this conversation with Roger. You have my word."

Arnie sighed. "Thanks. I really like my job. I wouldn't want to get, you know, fired." He winced as he spoke, then shook his head. "Your dad was a great man."

"Thank you," Jack said.

"He was patient and kind and really interested in all his employees. We all liked working for him and felt really bad when he died."

Jack nodded. He wasn't sure what to say when people talked about his father this way. They were describing someone he'd never met.

"Knock, knock."

He looked up and saw Samantha walking into his office. She looked from him to Arnie.

"Am I early or late?" she asked with a smile.

"Neither," he said. "Right on time. You're joining our meeting in progress."

Now that she had the job, she'd obviously decided there was no need to dress conservatively anymore—at least her definition of it. Gone were the black slacks and black-and-white jacket. In their place she wore a long skirt in a swirl of reds, greens and purples. A dark green sweater hung loosely past her hips. She had a patterned scarf draped over one shoulder, a half-dozen bracelets on each wrist and earrings that tinkled and swayed as she walked.

"This is Arnie," Jack said, pointing to the man sitting across from him at the conference table. "He's from IT. He'll be working with you on the Internet expansion. You tell him what you want and he'll tell you if it's possible. Arnie, this is Samantha."

The other man rose and wiped his palms on his jeans, then held out his hand. His mouth opened, closed, then opened again.

"Ah, hi," Arnie said, his eyes wide, his cheeks bright with color.

"Good morning." Samantha beamed at him. "So you're going to be my new best friend, right? And you won't ever want to tell me no."

Arnie stammered, then sank back in his seat. Jack did his best not to smile. Samantha had made another conquest.

He wasn't surprised. She walked into a room and men were instantly attracted to her. He was no exception. She was a weakness for which he'd found no antidote. Even now he found himself wanting to pull her close and run his hands through her curly hair. He wanted to stare into her eyes and feel her tremble in his embrace.

Not on this planet, he reminded himself. She hadn't been interested ten years ago and he doubted that had changed.

Okay, she'd been interested *once*. Apparently once was enough where he was concerned. She'd made it more than clear she didn't want a repeat performance.

"Don't let Samantha push you around," he told Arnie. "She has a tendency to do that."

Samantha looked at him and raised her eyebrows. "Me? Are you kidding? I'm the picture of complete cooperation."

"Uh-huh. Right until someone gets in your way. Then you're a steamroller."

Samantha sat next to Arnie and patted his hand. "Ignore him. Jack and I went to grad school together and he seems to remember things very differently. I've never steamrolled anyone." She paused, then smiled. "Well, at least not often. I can get tenacious about what I want, though. And I've read different reports from your department, Arnie. People have been pushing for this expansion for a while."

That surprised Jack. "I hadn't heard that."

Samantha looked at him. "His boss is the reason why. I also read memos from Roger explaining why it was all a bad idea. Apparently he had some backing on that."

She didn't specifically say by who, but Jack could guess. He doubted his father had been a fan of growing technology.

"That was the past," he said. "Let's focus on the future. You two need to get together and talk about specifics."

Samantha jotted down a note on her pad of paper. "I'll e-mail you, Arnie. You can let me know what works for you. I tend to put in long hours. I hope that's okay."

Arnie's pale eyes practically glowed. "It's fine. Sure. I'll be there." He stood and nodded. "Anytime. Just e-mail me."

"Thanks for your help," Jack said.

"Oh, yeah. No problem."

The other man left. Jack waited until the door closed, then turned to Samantha.

"You've made a friend."

"Arnie? He's very sweet, or so I've been told. I think we'll do fine together."

Jack told himself that she would never be interested in the other man and even if she was, it wasn't his business. He didn't care who Samantha wanted in her life as long as she did her job. He very nearly believed himself, too.

"What have you got?" he asked.

"Lots and lots of great ideas," she said with a smile. "I had an extremely productive weekend. I went over the existing Web site. It's pretty basic. There's so much room to improve and that's what I want. I want to start with kids twelve and under as our first target audience and I want to dazzle them."

She set a folder on the conference table and opened it. "We'll deal with the teens later, but first, let's get some buzz going. I want us to be the Web site the kids are dying to go to the second they get home from school. I want to do more than help them with their homework. I want us to be the coolest place on the Web. We can talk about sports and clothes and music. Movies, TV, trends. I was thinking we'd have an 'Ask Annie' kind of column."

He stared at her. "Who's Annie?"

She laughed. "I mean an advice column. Ask the resident expert. Annie, Mark, the name isn't important. But here's the cool part—it will be real-time and interactive. Like a chat room. I have a lot of ideas for developing all this. But our biggest concern is security. We're going to have to go state-of-the-art so the kids are totally safe on the Web site."

"I like it."

"Good."

Her smile widened and he felt it punch him right in the gut. Ever-present need growled to life.

"You don't need to run all this by me," he told her, doing his damnedest to ignore the blood rushing to his groin. "I trust you to run your department."

"I know, but this is big stuff. I'm talking about huge changes."

"That would be the reason I hired you."

She studied him. "You really trust me with all this?"

"Of course."

"Wow. Great. I guess I'll get my team to pull it all together and then we'll have a big presentation."

"I look forward to it." He leaned toward her. "That's how I run things, Samantha," he told her. "Until someone screws up, he or she has free rein."

"I would have thought you were more the control type."

"Because I wear a suit?"

"Sort of. You're a lawyer. That doesn't help with the image."

"What if I went into environmental law?"

She grinned. "Did you?"

"No. Criminal."

"So it's not just *suits*. It's designer suits."

"Mostly. But even at the law firm, I give my people room to grow and make mistakes. One screwup isn't fatal."

She tucked her hair behind her ear. "That sounds so balanced."

"I like to think of myself that way."

"You were less balanced in grad school. Much more…"

He looked at her. "Stick up the ass?"

Her mouth threatened a smile, but she held it back. "I would never have said that."

"But you were thinking it."

"Maybe a little. You had that study schedule."

"It kept me on track and freed up my weekends. I had plenty of time for fun."

"I remember," she said with a laugh. "Okay, I'll let it go. You weren't that rigid. I think you were just so much more together than any other guy I met. It scared me."

He wondered if that was true. Had he made her uneasy in ways he hadn't understood? Did it even matter now?

"You were the most unstructured successful person I'd met," he said.

"I was kind of crazy back then," she admitted. "I've calmed down some."

"I hope not. I liked you crazy. Remember the time we spent Christmas eve in a stable because you wanted to know what it was like?" he asked.

She laughed. "Yes, and you kept telling me that I needed to pay attention to geography."

"I was right. We were in Pennsylvania in the middle of winter. Not exactly the Middle East."

Despite the cold, they'd had a great time huddled together. He'd wanted her with a desperation that had made him tremble more than the cold. The next morning, he'd driven her to the airport so she could fly home to spend Christmas Day with her mother.

Speaking of which… "How's your mom?" he asked.

Samantha's smile faded. "She passed away about three years ago."

"I'm sorry," he said. "I really liked her."

"Thanks. I miss her. It was hard to lose her. She'd been sick for a while, so it wasn't a big surprise. We were able to say our goodbyes, which made things better." She collected her papers. "Okay, I'm going to let you get back to work. I have to put my presentation together so that you're dazzled, too. You will be, you know."

"I don't doubt it."

He walked her to the door, then returned to his desk. Only a crazy man would continue to want what he couldn't have, he told himself. Which made him certifiable. It was the human condition, he thought.

And now she'd caught Arnie in her web. Jack

could almost pity the guy. The difference was Arnie would probably fantasize about happily-ever-after while Jack only wanted Samantha in his bed. He'd learned a long time ago to concentrate on the physical and ignore the emotional. There was no point in engaging his heart—people who claimed to love quickly got over the feeling and then they left.

Samantha hadn't been sure what to expect when she'd signed up for "executive housing," but she was pleasantly surprised by all her condo had to offer. There was a spacious living room with a semi-view, a dining area and plenty of room in the kitchen, especially for someone who made it a point to dirty as few pots as possible.

Her bedroom held a king-size bed, a dresser and an armoire with a television. The closet was huge and she'd already soaked her troubles away in the massive whirlpool tub in her bathroom. There was even a workstation alcove with a desk for her laptop, good lighting and high-speed Internet connection.

The only downside to the space was the fact that it felt…impersonal. The neutral colors were so bland and the furniture so functional. There wasn't anything funky to be found.

Still, the condo worked for now and it was about double the size her New York apartment had been. As she stood in front of the slider leading out to her small balcony and con-sidered take-out options for dinner, she felt a whisper of contentment steal over her.

Coming to Chicago had been a good idea, she thought. She'd needed to leave New York. Despite loving the city, there were too many Vance memories around, and she'd needed to get away from them and him. Here she could start over. Build new memories. There were—

Someone knocked on her door. She crossed the beige carpet and looked through the peephole.

"Jack?" she asked as she pulled open the door.

"I'm presuming," he said, holding up two brown bags. "I come bearing Chinese food. I have wine, too. Sort of a welcome-to-the-building thing. Interested?"

She was delighted, she thought, stepping back and motioning him to enter. Instead, a black-and-white border collie slipped by Jack and stepped into the apartment.

"This is Charlie," Jack said. "Do you like dogs?"

Samantha held out her fingers for Charlie to sniff, then petted him. "I love them." She crouched down in front of Charlie and rubbed his shoulders. "Who's a handsome guy?" she asked, then laughed as he tried to lick her face.

"He likes you," Jack said. "Smart dog."

She laughed. "Okay, now I *really* want to have dinner with you. Come on in."

She led the way to the kitchen where Jack opened the wine and she collected plates for their dinner. As she opened the bags and began pulling out cartons of food, she noticed a bright red plastic bowl and a box with a big *C* on it.

"This is interesting," she said, holding up both.

Jack grinned sheepishly. "They're for Charlie. He loves Chinese, so the place I go mixes up a special rice dish for him. It's beef and chicken, rice, vegetables, light on the salt and spices. He loves it and the vet approves. It's kind of a special treat."

Samantha did her best to reconcile the strait-laced lawyer she knew Jack to be with a guy who would special order food for his dog.

"Now I know who's really in charge," she murmured.

"Yeah," Jack said easily. "He's the boss."

He helped her carry the cartons to the table. Charlie was served, but he waited until they sat down before digging in to his dinner.

Jack held out his glass of wine. "Welcome to the neighborhood. I hope you like it."

"Thank you." They touched glasses, then she took a sip of the red wine. "Very nice. All of this."

"No problem. I thought you might still be feeling out of place."

"Some. I like the apartment, but it's weird because nothing in here is mine. Like these plates." She held up the plain cream plate. "I would never have bought these."

"Too normal?"

"Too boring. Color is our friend."

"Agreed. But you'll get settled, then you can find a place of your own."

"I know. But for now, this is great. They make it very convenient."

Jack passed her the honey-glazed shrimp. "That's why I'm here. Dry cleaning right downstairs. The corner grocery store delivers. The dog walker lives across the street. There are over twenty restaurants in a five-block square around here and a great park close by where Charlie and I hang out on weekends."

She glanced at the dog who had finished his dinner and was now sniffing the floor for rice grains he might have missed. "He's beautiful. But doesn't he need exercise and attention? You're a guy who works long hours."

"He's fine," Jack said. "Is it quiet enough here for you? That's the first thing I noticed when I moved in. How quiet it was. Good construction."

She started to agree, then realized he had not-so-subtly changed the subject. "It's great," she said. "What aren't you telling me?"

He looked at her and raised his eyebrows. "I don't know what you mean."

"About Charlie. You changed the subject."

"From what?"

"How he gets through the day without tearing up your place."

"He keeps busy."

Jack looked uncomfortable. She glanced from him to the dog. "What? He watches soaps and does a crossword puzzle?"

Jack sighed. "He goes to day care, okay? I know, I know. It's silly, but he has a lot of energy and border collies are herding dogs. I didn't want him alone and bored all the time so three days a week he goes to doggy day care. There he plays with the other dogs and herds them around. He comes home so tired that on Tuesdays and Thursdays he pretty much just sleeps. I have a dog walker who comes by twice a day to take him out."

The muscles in his jaw tensed slightly as he spoke. She could tell he hadn't wanted to share that part of his life with her.

She did her best not to smile or laugh—he would take that wrong—not realizing that women would find a big, tough, successful guy who cared that much about his dog pretty appealing.

"You're a responsible pet owner," she said. "Some people aren't."

He narrowed his gaze, as if waiting for a

slam. She smiled innocently, then changed the subject.

After dinner they moved to the living room. Charlie made a bid for the wing chair in the corner. Jack ordered him out of it. The dog gave a sigh of long suffering, then stretched out on the carpet by Samantha.

Jack glanced around at the furniture, then studied the painting over the fireplace. "So not you," he said.

Samantha looked at the subtle blues and greens. "It's very restful."

"You hate it."

"I wouldn't have gone for something so…"

"Normal?" he asked.

She grinned. "Exactly. Too expected. Where's the interesting furniture, the splash of color?"

"I'm sure you'll do that with your next place."

"Absolutely. I miss fringe."

He winced. "I remember you had that horrible shawl over that table in your apartment when we were in grad school. It was the ugliest thing I'd ever seen."

"It was beautiful," she told him. "And it had an amazing color palate."

"It looked like something from a Dali nightmare."

"You have no taste," she said.

"I know when to be afraid."

He smiled as he spoke, making her own mouth curve up in return. It had always been like this, she thought. They rarely agreed and yet they got along just fine. She liked that almost as much as she liked looking at him.

He'd changed out of his workday suit into jeans and a long-sleeved shirt. The denim had seen better days. Dozens of washings had softened and faded the material, molding to his long legs and narrow hips.

A controlled sex appeal, she thought. Reined-in power that always made her wonder what would happen when he lost control. How big would the explosion be? She had an idea from their lone night together. He had claimed her with a need that had left her shaking and desperately wanting more.

Step *away* from the memory, she told herself. Talk about dangerous territory.

"Don't you have some furniture and decorations from your New York apartment?" he asked.

"I have a few things in storage," she said. A very few things. In an ongoing attempt to control her, Vance had fought her over every picture and dish. It had been easier and oddly freeing simply to walk away.

An emotion flickered in his dark eyes. "I know you're coming off of a divorce. How are you holding up?"

The news wasn't a secret, so she wasn't surprised that he knew. "Okay. It was tough at first. I went through the whole 'I've failed' bit, but I've moved on from that. Right now I'm feeling a lot of relief."

"It's a tough time," he said.

She nodded. "I had really planned to stay married to the same man for the rest of my life. I thought I'd picked the perfect guy." She paused. "Not perfect. Perfect for me. But I was wrong."

An understatement, she thought grimly. "We wanted different things in nearly everything. I could have lived with that, but he changed his mind about wanting children." She kept her voice light because if she gave in to her real feelings, the bitterness would well up inside of her. She didn't want to deal with that right now. Talk about a waste of energy.

"I'm sorry," Jack said. "I remember you used to talk about having kids all the time."

"I still plan to have them. I think I have a few good years left."

"More than a few."

She smiled as she spoke. Jack liked the way she curled up on the sofa, yet kept one leg lowered so she could rub Charlie with her bare foot.

She still painted her toenails, he thought, looking at the tiny flowers painted on each big toe. She even had a toe ring on each foot. None of the women he got involved with were the toe-ring type. Of course none of them wore jeans with flowers sewn onto the side seams or sweaters that looked more like a riot of colors than clothing.

"Enough about me," she said. "What have you been up to, romantically?"

"Nothing that interesting," he told her. "No wives, current or ex. I was engaged for a while."

"Oh. It didn't work out?"

"She died."

Samantha's eyes widened. "Jack, I'm sorry."

"Thanks. It was a few years ago, just before Christmas. Shelby's car spun out on an icy bridge and went into the water. She didn't make it."

"How horrible."

Samantha was the sympathetic type. She would want to say the right thing, only to realize there wasn't one. He'd heard all the platitudes possible and none of them had made a damn bit of difference. Not after he'd found Shelby's note. The one she'd written before she'd died.

"Was it very close to the wedding?" she asked.

"Just a little over a week. We were planning to get married New Year's Eve."

She bit her lower lip. "You must hate the holidays now."

"Not as much as I would have thought. I get angry, thinking about what was lost."

Not for him and Shelby—he'd done his best to let that go—but for her family. They were good people and he knew they'd yet to move on.

"Relationships are never easy," she said.

Charlie chose that moment to roll onto his back and offer his stomach for rubbing. Samantha obliged him and he started to groan.

"That dog knows a good thing when he has one," Jack said.

She looked at him and grinned. "Oh, right. Because *you* don't spoil him."

"Me? Never." He sipped on his wine. "Are you overwhelmed by work yet?"

"Almost. Ask me again in two days and I'm sure the answer will be yes. There's so much to do, and that's what makes it all exciting. This is a great opportunity."

He was glad she thought so. He wanted energetic people solving company problems as quickly as possible. "Have you heard about the big advertiser party? It's in a few weeks. It's an annual function and very upscale. Formal attire required."

"Really? You mean I have an excuse to buy a new dress and look fabulous?"

The thought of her in something long and slinky suddenly made him look forward to the party in ways he hadn't before. "It's not just an excuse," he said. "It's an order."

"And you'll be in a tux?"

He grimaced. "Oh, yeah."

"I'm sure you'll look great. All the women will be fawning over you."

"Fawning gets old," he said, doing his best not to read anything into her comment. While he wanted to believe she was flirting, he'd been shot down enough in the past to know that wishful thinking got him exactly nowhere.

"Do you have a lot of it?" she asked, her green eyes sparkling with humor.

"Enough."

"And just how much is that?"

He sensed they were in dangerous territory, but he wasn't sure how to avoid getting in trouble.

"I date," he said cautiously.

"I would guess that you have women lining up to be with you," she said easily. "You're good-looking, successful, well-off and single. That's fairly irresistible."

Except for Samantha, that had always been

his take on it, too. So why did he get the feeling that she didn't see the list as a good thing?

"Some women manage to resist," he said. "What about you? Ready to start dating?"

"I don't think so. Not for a while. Divorce has a way of sucking the confidence out of a person. Or at least it did me."

He couldn't believe that. She had always been confident. Smart, funny, gorgeous. "It doesn't show."

She smiled. "Thanks. I'm getting by on sheer determination."

"It's working."

He wanted to tell her she had nothing to worry about—that she was as desirable as ever and he was willing to prove it.

Not a good idea, he reminded himself. So instead of speaking, or acting, he stood. "It's late. Charlie and I need our beauty sleep." He whistled softly. "Come on, boy."

Charlie rose and stretched. He licked Samantha's hand, then joined Jack.

She got up and followed them to the front door. "Thanks for stopping by. Dinner was great. I appreciated the company, as well." She crouched down and rubbed Charlie's ears. "You're a very handsome boy. We'll have to get together again soon."

Charlie barked his agreement.

Figures, Jack thought with a grin. After all these years, she falls for the dog.

Chapter Three

Nearly a week later, Jack sat behind what had been his father's desk, cursing his agreement to take over the company, even temporarily. Every day brought a new crisis and, with it, bad news. At this point all he was asking for was twenty-four hours without something major going wrong.

He'd already had to deal with the IT people informing him that their Web pages were nearly at capacity and, to support the Web expansion, they were going to have to negotiate with their server. The previous quarter's report showed magazine subscriptions falling for their three best publications. A train derailment had destroyed nearly a hundred thousand magazines heading to the West Coast markets and he'd just seen the layout for the launch of their new home-decorating magazine and even he could tell it sucked the big one.

There was too much to deal with, he thought. How the hell had his father done all this *and* run several departments?

Jack leaned back in his chair and rubbed his temples. He already had the answer to that one—George Hanson hadn't done it well. Things had slipped and there'd been no time to fix them before the next crisis had appeared. Despite hiring department heads, Jack was still overwhelmed by the sheer volume of work.

As far as he could tell, there was only one way for Hanson Media Group to survive—he had to get more help.

He buzzed for his assistant. When Mrs. Wycliff entered his office, he motioned for her to take a seat.

"I need to get in touch with my brothers," he said. "Do you know where Evan and Andrew are these days?"

If the older woman was surprised that Jack didn't know where to find his brothers himself, she didn't show it.

"I'm sorry, I don't," she said. "Would you like me to try to find them?"

"Please. I suggest you follow the credit-card charges. That's generally the easiest way." Evan favored Europe and Andrew tended to follow the seasons—summering in exclusive beach resorts and wintering in places like Whistler and Gstaad.

Jack knew all the psychobabble about siblings. In every family each tried to get his parents' attention in a different way. For Jack, it had been about being the best at whatever he did. He'd learned early that he was expected to take over the family business and for a long time he'd worked toward that. But in the end, he'd walked away from Hanson Media Group, just like his brothers.

None of them had made the old man proud.

Did Evan and Andrew ever feel guilty? Jack had tried to make peace with his father more than once, but the old man had never seemed interested. All he'd talked about was how Jack should be at Hanson Media Group instead of practicing law.

Jack regretted losing touch with his brothers a lot more than he regretted disappointing his father.

"I'll get right on that," Mrs. Wycliff told him. "Have you spoken with your uncle?"

"Not about this," Jack told her. "But that's a great idea. Thank you."

She rose. "I'll let you know as soon as I locate them," she said, then left.

Jack buzzed David's office. "Hi. Are you available?"

"Absolutely."

The public relations department was the next floor down, on the main level of Hanson Media Group. Here the bright overhead lights contrasted with the rich blues and purples in the carpet and on the sofas and chairs.

Jack took the stairs and made his way to David's office. His uncle couldn't have been more different from Jack's father. Where George had lived and breathed business, David always had time for his nephews.

David's secretary waved him in. Jack pushed open the door and walked into David's large office.

The space had been designed to impress and put people at ease. It did both. David walked around his desk and shook hands with Jack, then pulled him close for a quick hug.

"How's it going?" David asked as he led the

way to the sofas in the corner. "Still finding things wrong?"

"Every day. I'm hoping for some good news soon. I figure we're all due."

"Toward the end, George wasn't himself," David said. "I think the work became too much for him. I'm guessing. He didn't confide in me."

"Did he confide in anyone?" Jack asked.

"Probably not. You hanging in there?"

"Do I have a choice?"

Jack looked at his uncle. Like all the Hanson men, he was tall, with brown hair. His eyes were lighter and he was nearly twenty years younger than his brother. Maybe that was why David had always been closer to his nephews. Maybe that was why David had been able to be there for them, Jack thought. George had been more like a father than a brother to David.

"You always have a choice," David told him. "You could walk."

"I gave my word to the board. I'm here for three months to clear things up and then I'm gone. I'm trying to get ahold of Evan and Andrew."

David frowned. "Good luck with that."

"Mrs. Wycliff is going to follow the money. That always works." Jack shook his head. "They should be here. We should do this together."

"You've never been close. Why expect it now?"

"Good point." Jack didn't have an answer. "Who am I kidding? If I had the chance to bolt, I'd take it."

"No, you wouldn't," David said. "You could have told the board no and you didn't. You have a strong sense of responsibility."

"Great. Look where it got me—here."

"Is that so bad?"

"It's keeping me from my real job." Jack leaned forward. "Why don't you take over? You know more about Hanson Media Group than any of us. You could run the company."

"Not my thing," David said. "Even if it was,

I would respect my brother's wishes. He wanted one of his sons to be in charge."

"We don't know that," Jack said. "And we won't until the will is read." He swore. "What was my father thinking? Why on earth would he want us to wait three months to read the will? It's crazy. Nothing can be settled until then. For all we know, he's giving his majority shares to the cat."

David grinned. "He didn't have a cat."

Someone knocked on the door. "Come in," David called.

His secretary walked in with a tray and set it on the coffee table. "Anything else?"

David smiled at her. "Thanks, Nina. You didn't have to do this."

"No problem. Oh, you had a call from the printers."

David groaned. "I don't want to know, do I?"

"Not really," Nina said cheerfully. "Don't worry. I've already fixed the problem."

With that she left.

Jack reached for one of the cups of coffee. "Tell me Andrew and Evan will at least come back for the reading of the will."

David looked at him. "Are you hoping to cut and run the second their plane touches down?"

"It crossed my mind. I have a law practice to get back to."

"Maybe you'll appreciate your career more if you have to suffer a little here," his uncle told him.

Jack narrowed his gaze. "If you start talking about Zen centering, I'm going to have to punch you."

David laughed. "You know what I mean. You shouldn't take things for granted."

"I don't. I'm not here to learn a life lesson. My father convinced the board that I was the only possible heir and now they're pressuring me to take over. It's all about self-interest. His, theirs, mine. My father didn't give a damn about what I wanted. He's doing his best to control me from the grave."

"George loved you," David said. "In his own way."

"That's like saying the black widow spider doesn't mean it personally when she kills her mate." He took another drink of coffee. "You've always defended him, even as you stepped in to take his place as our father."

David shrugged. "I wanted to help."

"You should have had a family of your own."

"So should you. Speaking of which, I put out a press release about the new people you've hired. One of the names was familiar."

"Samantha was the best person for the job," Jack said, refusing to get defensive.

"I don't doubt that. I'm simply saying it was interesting to see her name again. I remember her from your time in grad school. The one who got away."

"She was never that," Jack told him.

"You talked about her as if she were."

"That was a long time ago. Things are different now."

"Is she married?"

"No."

"Then maybe fate is giving you a second chance."

Jack looked at his uncle. "If you start drinking herbal tea next, we're going to have to have a talk."

David chuckled. "I'm just saying maybe you're getting a second chance."

"I don't believe in them."

David's humor faded and he gave Jack a serious look. "Not every woman is Shelby."

"I know that." He put down his coffee and stood. "Don't worry about me. I'm fine. As for Samantha, she's a co-worker, nothing more."

David grinned. "You're lying. But we'll play your game and pretend you're not."

"Gee, thanks. And if you hear anything on the whereabouts of my brothers, let me know."

"You'll be the first."

* * *

"Oh, my," Helen said as she looked around the condo. "It's very…"

"Plain? Beige? Boring?" Samantha asked with a grin.

"I was going to say very 'not you.' But those will work as well." She stepped forward and hugged Samantha again. "I'm so glad you're here."

"Me, too. Getting out of New York was number one on my to-do list. You made that happen."

Helen sank onto the sofa and dismissed Samantha with a flick of her wrist. "Oh, please. I got you an interview. I certainly didn't get you hired. It's not as if Jack would ever think to ask my opinion of anything. You got the job on your own."

Samantha settled next to her friend and touched her arm. "You look tired. How do you feel?"

"Exhausted. Shell-shocked. It's been two months. I guess I should be used to it by now, but I'm not." Tears filled her eyes, but Helen blinked them away. "Damn. I promised myself I was done with crying."

"There's no time limit on grief."

"I know." Helen squeezed her fingers. "You're sweet to worry about me. I'm fine."

"No, you're not."

"Okay. I'm pretending to be fine and that should count for something. Most of the time I do okay. I can now go for an hour or two without falling apart. In the beginning I was only able to survive minutes. So that's an improvement. It's just I miss him so much and I feel so alone."

Samantha didn't know what to say. Helen really *was* alone in all this. She didn't have any family of her own and George's sons hadn't exactly welcomed her with open arms.

"Have you tried talking to Jack?" she asked. "He's not unreasonable."

"I know," Helen said as she dug in her purse.

She pulled out a tissue and wiped under her eyes. "He's very polite and concerned, but we're not close. I tried. I tried so hard, but no matter what I did, those boys resisted." She sniffed. "I suppose I shouldn't call them boys. They're all grown men. They were grown when I met them. It's just that's how George thought of them. As his boys."

Samantha angled toward her friend. "I don't get it, either. They should have adored you."

"Oh, I agree. I did everything I could think of. On my good days, I tell myself it wasn't me. George was a wonderful man, but he was never very close with his sons. I don't know why. Whatever problems they had existed long before he met me. Oh, but I loved him so much."

"I know you did."

Helen smiled. "All right. This is stupid. I didn't come here to cry. I want to talk about you. Tell me everything. Are you loving your job?"

Samantha accepted the change in subject. She didn't know how to help her friend, so maybe distracting her would allow her a few minutes away from the pain.

"Every second," she said. "There's so much work, which is great. I like keeping busy. I have so many ideas for the new Web site that I've started keeping a pad of paper and a pen on the nightstand. I wake up two or three times a night with more details or directions or things we could do."

Helen wrinkled her nose. "I can see we're going to have to have the 'balance' conversation in a few weeks."

"Maybe," Samantha said with a laugh. "But for now, I'm really happy. I like the people I work with, I feel I'm contributing. It's great."

"Do you miss Vance?"

Samantha sighed. "No. And I really mean it. I thought I'd hurt more, but I think all the betrayal burned away the love. For the longest time I thought I'd never forgive him. Lately, I've come to see that I don't care enough to worry about forgiveness. He was horrible in so many ways. I have to think about myself and getting better. Not about him."

"Good for you. You've made a fresh start. You can get back on your feet. Look around. Maybe fall in love again."

Samantha held up her fingers in the sign of a cross. "Get back. There will be no talk of love or relationships in the context of my life, thank you very much." She lowered her hands to her lap. "I'm done with men."

"Forever?"

"For a while. I don't need the pain and suffering."

"It's not all like that," Helen said. "Vance wasn't the one for you. You figured that out and moved on. It was the right thing to do. But you don't want to turn your back on love. You don't want to miss the chance to have a great love. I believe there's one great love for everyone."

Samantha nodded. "And George was yours."

"He was everything," Helen said. "I was so lucky to find him. We shared so much. That's what I want to remember forever. How much we shared. How much we mattered to each other. I'll never find that again."

Samantha wondered if that was true. Helen was still a relatively young woman. And a beautiful one. Samantha had a feeling there was at least one other great love in her friend's life. As for herself, she wasn't interested in trying. Not when she'd been burned so badly.

"Speaking of men," Helen said. "What's it like working with Jack?"

"Good. He's very efficient and gives me all the room I need."

Helen raised her eyebrows. "And?"

Samantha shrugged. "And what?"

"Are there sparks? I remember there were sparks when you were in grad school with him. I remember long discussions about whether or not you should risk getting involved with him. I also remember saying you should, but you ignored me."

"He's not my type," she said, sidestepping the sparks question. Mostly because she didn't want to admit they were still there and starting fires every time she and Jack were in the same room.

"Type doesn't always enter into it," Helen said. "Some men simply turn us on."

"If you say so."

Her friend stared at her. "Jack isn't like Vance. He's honest and he's been hurt."

Samantha drew back. She was beginning to think all men were like Vance. "Are you matchmaking? If so, stop right now. It's so not allowed."

"I'm not. I'm making a point. Jack's a great guy."

"For someone else."

"If you say so."

* * *

Jack's last meeting finished at four. He returned to his office and found several empty boxes by the wall.

Mrs. Wycliff, efficient as ever, had delivered them while he'd been out. He planned to pack up a lot of his father's things and have them put in storage until his brothers showed up. Then the three of them could sit down with Helen and figure out who wanted what and what to do with anything left over.

He headed for the bookcase first. There were several out-of-date directories and registries. He dropped those into boxes without a second glance, then slowed when he came to the pictures of his father with various clients, city leaders and employees.

"No pictures of family," Jack murmured. No graduation shots, no informal photos taken on vacation or over holidays. Probably because they'd never much traveled as a family and, after his mother's death, holidays had been grim, dutiful affairs at best.

It should have been different, he thought. He knew guys with brothers and they were all tight. Why hadn't he, Evan and Andrew connected? Why weren't they close? They were all dealing with the death of their father. Wouldn't they do it better together?

"Did it matter? I don't even know where they are."

What did that say about the relationship? That he had no idea where to find either of his brothers? Nothing good.

He finished with the bookcase and started on the credenza. He needed room to store reports, quarterly statements and the like. The credenza was perfect. He pulled out old files and glanced through them. Some of them were over a decade old. Was that what had gone wrong with the company? Had his father been unable to stay focused on the present?

Jack had a feeling he would never get those questions answered. He and his father had never been close and any opportunity for that had been lost years ago. What made the situation even worse was Jack could barely feel regret about the circumstances.

He filled more boxes with papers, files and bound reports. When the credenza was empty, he reached for the quarterly reports and started to slide them in place. But the shelf wasn't high enough.

"That doesn't make sense," he said as he looked at the credenza. "They should fit."

He reached inside and poked around, only to realize the base of the shelf was too thick by a couple of inches. What the hell?

After a little more prodding, he felt a narrow piece of metal, almost like a lever. When he pushed on it, the shelf popped up revealing a long, shallow recessed space and a set of leather books.

Jack's first thought was that his father had kept a diary. He was surprised to find himself anxious to read the older man's thoughts. But when he picked up the first book and flipped through it, there weren't any personal notes. Instead he stared at rows and rows of numbers.

His world was the law and it took him a second to realize he was looking at a detailed income statement. He glanced at the date and felt his stomach clench. This was for the previous year. He'd just spent the better part of the morning looking at the income statement for the past year. He was familiar with those numbers and they weren't anything like these.

Even though he already knew, he still found the first statement and compared it to the one his father had kept hidden. All the entry titles were the same but the amounts were different, and not for the better.

Anger filled him. Anger and a growing sense of betrayal. George Hanson had kept the truth from everyone. Jack didn't know how he'd done it, but the proof was here in the second set of books he'd hidden away.

Not only was the company close to bankruptcy, but his father's concealment had been criminal and premeditated. The company was totally screwed—and so was Jack.

Chapter Four

Jack carefully went through the books, hoping to find something to show that he'd been wrong—that his father *hadn't* defrauded employees, stockholders and his family. But with every column, every total, the truth became more impossible to avoid.

He stood and crossed to the window where the night sky of Chicago stretched out before him. He could feel the walls closing in and fought against the sense of being trapped. With news like this, the board would pressure him to stay longer. They would insist that a three-month commitment to get things straightened out simply wasn't enough. In their position, he would do the same.

He heard someone knock on his office door, then push it open. He turned toward the sound.

"You're working late," Samantha said as she walked toward him. "I had a feeling you would still be here. You executive types—always going the extra mile. Doesn't being so conscientious get—" She stopped in mid-stride and stared at him. "What's wrong?"

So much for a poker face, he thought grimly. There was no point in keeping the truth from her. He would be calling an emergency board meeting first thing in the morning. Time was critical. The financial information would have to be disclosed, first to the board, and then to the investors and the financial world. His father had insisted on taking the company public, which meant playing by the rules of the SEC.

"I found a second set of books," he said, nodding toward his desk. "My father kept them by hand. I've checked them against the computer financial statements and they don't add up. He was concealing massive expenditures and losses."

Samantha's eyes widened. "Fraud?"

"That's one word for it. I can think of fifty others. We're going to have to do a complete audit and find out the true financial situation. I doubt it's going to be good news. We're talking about a possible SEC investigation, plenty of bad press and downturn in the stock price." He returned his attention to the view. "At least the family owns a majority of the shares. We don't have to worry about a total sell-off. There will be a hit in our price, but it shouldn't be too bad. Not with a new management team in place and complete disclosure."

"I don't know what to say," she admitted.

"You and me, both. Not exactly what you want to hear about your new employer. Ready to cut and run?"

"What? Of course not." She moved next to him. "Are you all right?"

"I'm not happy, if that's what you mean. Just once, I'd like to be surprised by good news."

"Jack, you're talking about your father. That he concealed material financial information. That's a big deal."

"Good thing he's dead, then. Otherwise, he'd be going to jail."

He sounded so calm, Samantha thought. As if all this were happening to someone else. From what she knew, Jack and his father had never been tight, but this had to be hard for him. No one wanted to find out a parent had committed a crime.

"He wasn't a bad man," she said, not knowing if there was any way to make this easier for Jack. "Maybe he just got in over his head."

He looked at her. "You're trying to justify what he did?"

"Of course not. But from everything I've heard, he wasn't evil."

"He doesn't have to be evil to have broken the law. People do it all the time." He shook his head. "I'm almost not surprised. He ran several departments himself. He couldn't give up the control. Maybe this was just another way of holding on tight. The numbers weren't what he wanted them to be, so he modified them. No wonder he wasn't big on change—technology would have made it tough for him to hide the truth."

"But he did," she said.

"In spades. I wonder if David knows about this?"

"Are you going to ask him?"

"I'm going to ask everyone," Jack said. "The only way to ward off a crisis is to have a plan in place to solve the problem and to find anyone who may have helped him."

"You don't think he acted alone?"

"Unlikely. But I know it was his idea."

"You might want to talk to Helen," Samantha said before she could stop herself. "She may know something."

Jack glanced at her. "You think she was involved?"

"What? No! Helen wouldn't do anything like this. But she might be able to tell you if George was acting stressed or if he suddenly seemed to change. She might have some suggestions."

His mouth twisted. "I don't need shopping advice."

Samantha stiffened at the insult to her friend. "Is that what you think of her? That she's a useless bimbo who only cares about clothes and jewelry?"

He shrugged. "I don't really know the woman."

"And why is that? She's been a part of this family for a while now. Why weren't you interested in even trying to get to know her?"

"I'm familiar with the type."

"Helen isn't a type. She's a person and she's not the person you imagine her to be. How interesting. You think your father got himself and the company in this position because he held on too tight to outdated ideas. It seems to me that you're a lot like that, too."

Samantha took notes as one of her team members wrapped up his presentation. "Great job, Phil," she said. "I really like how you're using colors to coordinate your section. It will make navigating the site really fun."

"Younger kids respond to colors. They're easier for them than instructions," he said with a grin. "I was thinking we could use the same format for the sections for older kids, but with the colors getting darker. Light blue flowing into dark blue into navy. So clicking on anything blue will automatically pop up math-related questions."

"Good idea," she told him, then looked at Arnie. "So, does that make your job harder or easier?"

Arnie rubbed his hand on his khakis. "Once we get it programmed, it's not a problem."

"Good." She found it helpful always to include the IT guys in on the planning stages of any Internet project. Better to get their cooperation and input while the work was still easily modified.

"You could, ah, use drop-down menus, too," Arnie said. "After they click on the color. So it's not just one question. It could be a series. And then based on how they answer, they can go to another place on the site. Like if they get the answer right, they get a mini game. You know, for motivation."

Samantha glanced at her team, who all seemed pleased with the idea.

"Good thinking," she said. "You have a big thumbs-up on that one, Arnie. Thanks."

He shrugged and blushed. His gaze never left her face.

Samantha recognized the signs of a crush and wasn't exactly sure what to do about it. Not only wasn't she looking for love right now, Arnie wasn't her type. He was a nice enough guy, but nothing about him caused her to tingle.

Just then the conference-room door opened and Jack stepped inside. He didn't say anything and quietly took a seat in the back.

Instantly her body went on alert, just in case her brain hadn't noticed his arrival. She hated that even though she was still angry with him, she reacted physically. She found herself wanting to sit up straighter and push out her chest. Of course the complete lack of significant breast-type curves made that gesture futile, but still, the urge to flaunt was there.

Go figure, she thought. Arnie was available and pleasant and smart and probably completely uncomplicated. Nothing about him pushed any of her emotional buttons. Jack might be available and sexy, but he was also her worst-case scenario, man-wise, and totally unreasonable. He made her crazy with his assumptions about Helen.

Which they would deal with another time, she thought as she turned her attention back to the meeting in progress.

"The reward games should be related to the topic," Sandy said. "At least on some level. Like a blaster game based on times tables for the math color or something scientific for the science section."

"The difficulty of the games could increase with each grade level," Phil added.

"We're going to be spending a lot of time on content," Samantha said. "But it will be worth it. We'll need to take these ideas to research and get them going on questions and answers. We can do timed and non-timed quizzes. Maybe coordinate some of the questions with what's being studied in the textbooks. Are they standardized by region? Let's find that out. If we can emphasize what they're already studying, we'll reinforce the teachers' lessons."

"I'm working on the time line," Jeff said. "So a kid can type in a date and find out what's happening all over the world at that time. We're thinking anything date related will reference back to the time line. So if someone is working on a paper on Thomas Jefferson and they go online for information, the Web site will offer a time-line link. That way the student can see not only what was happening in this country, but everywhere. We can also cross-reference, so with the Jefferson paper, they could talk about what was happening in China and how it was the same but different."

"Wish I'd had that when I was in school," Samantha said.

"Me, too," Jeff said. "I would have done better in history."

The meeting continued. Ideas were offered and discussed. They had a limited amount of time to get the Web site up and running, so there would be a final of only the best. Still, she wanted as much to choose from as possible.

As people spoke and offered suggestions, Samantha was careful not to look at Jack. On the professional side, she knew it was important to put their argument behind them. As someone who cared about her friend, she was still really mad.

"That should take care of it for now," she said. "Good work, people. I'm impressed. We'll meet again on Friday."

Her staff stood and headed for the door. Arnie glanced at Jack, who remained seated at the table. The smaller man hesitated, looked at her, then left. Samantha had no choice but to acknowledge her boss.

"We're getting there," she said as she collected her notes.

"Yes, you are," he told her. "Your team works well together. I like where things are going."

"Good."

"You have an easy working style. You're firmly in charge, but you don't force your will on anyone."

"What's the point of that?" she asked. "I already know what I think. I'm looking for their ideas."

"Not everyone thinks that way."

She didn't know what to say to that.

"You're still mad at me," he said, making it a statement not a question, so she had no reason to deny it.

"I don't understand why you're determined to think the worst of Helen. From what I can tell, you barely know the woman. If you'd spent time with her and she'd been horrible, I would understand your less-than-flattering opinion. But you're basing it all on a few casual meetings and the mythology that stepmothers are inherently evil."

One corner of his mouth twitched. "It's not about her being my stepmother."

"Then what is it?"

He hesitated. "She's much younger than my father," he began. "My father was not a kind man."

Samantha stood. "Oh, I see. You're saying she married him for his money? Is that it?" Anger filled her. "I've known Helen for years. In fact, she used to be my babysitter. We've stayed close. She's like family to me. She loved your father. Maybe you and he didn't get along so you're having trouble with that concept, but it's true. She considers him the love of her life. I can't help defending her. It's like you're attacking my sister."

Jack rose. "You seem very sincere."

"I am."

They stared at each other. His dark gaze never wavered. At last he shrugged. "Then you must be right."

She nearly collapsed back in her chair. "What?"

"You've never lied to me, Samantha. I knew you pretty well back in grad school. You were never dishonest and you weren't stupid about people. So I'll respect your opinion on Helen."

Okay, she heard the words, but they didn't make sense to her. "What does that mean, exactly?"

"That you believe she's a good person. You're right, I haven't spent much time with her. I don't know the woman at all. Maybe she's nothing I've imagined."

Just like that? She studied him, looking for some hint that he was toying with her, but she couldn't find it. And to use his own words, she'd known *him* pretty well back in grad school and he hadn't been a liar, either. A little rigid maybe, but that was hardly a crime. Not that he'd done anything to admit *he* might be wrong in this case.

"Okay, then," she said. "That's good."

"So we're not fighting anymore?" he asked.

"I guess not."

"You sound disappointed."

"I have a lot of energy floating around inside of me," she admitted. "I'm not sure how to burn it off."

The second she said the words, his body stiffened. Tension filled the room and it had nothing to do with them not getting along. Every inch of her became aware of every inch of him and some of those inches were especially appealing.

Her mind screamed for her to run as far and as fast as she could. Her body begged her to stay and take advantage of the situation.

He broke the spell by glancing at his watch. "I have to prepare for the board meeting tomorrow."

"Is everyone flying in for it?" she asked.

"Most. A couple will tap in by phone. It's not going to be pretty."

She couldn't begin to imagine how that conversation would go. "I checked the papers this morning. There wasn't a leak."

He shrugged. "I didn't expect there to be. As of eight last night, only you and I knew."

"Oh." She'd assumed there were more people in the loop. "I didn't say anything to anyone."

"I knew you wouldn't."

With that, he excused himself and left. Samantha sank back in her chair and waited for the ache inside to fade.

What was it about Jack that got to her? He was everything she didn't like in a man—well-off, controlling, powerful. And yet he'd just said he was wrong about Helen. In all the years they'd been married, Vance had never once made a mistake—at least in his mind. Certainly not one he would admit to. So in that respect the two men were different.

But it wasn't enough, she thought. And she couldn't take a chance on making another mistake like the last one. If she did, the next one could kill her.

* * *

Three of the board members lived in the Chicago area. Two flew in and two would be on speakerphone. Mrs. Wycliff arranged for coffee and sandwiches, but Jack doubted anyone would be in the mood to eat. Not when the news was this bad.

He waited until exactly eleven-thirty, then walked into the boardroom. The five people standing there turned to look at him.

He knew a couple by sight, having met them at various functions. The other three introduced themselves, then introduced the two who hadn't been able to make the meeting. The chairman, a craggy man in his late sixties named Baynes, motioned for everyone to take a seat. Jack found himself sitting at one end of the long conference table, while Baynes took the other. Jack had filled each of them in by phone so now they could get right to it.

"Sorry business," the older man said. "How did it happen?"

Everyone looked at Jack. "I have no idea," he said. "Until you asked me to step in for my late father, I'd been busy with my law practice."

"He never talked about the business with you? Never mentioned how things were going?"

"No." Jack didn't see any point in explaining he and his father had never spoken much at all, about the company or anything. He set the second set of books on the conference table. "I found these when I was cleaning out his credenza. There was a false bottom on one of the shelves. He didn't want anyone to find them."

He pushed the books to the center of the table. No one seemed to want to be the first to touch them. Finally Baynes motioned for them and the lone woman on the board pushed them in his general direction.

"The chief financial officer has made copies of everything," Jack said. "She's already running the numbers to find out where we really are. We should have some accurate information by the end of the week."

"The auditors are going to have hell to pay," Baynes said absently.

Jack nodded. Every publicly traded company was required by law to be audited by an independent accounting firm. Somehow George's double books had gotten past them.

But their problems were the least of Jack's concerns. "I've prepared a statement," he said. "We'll issue it after the board meeting."

Several of the board members looked at each other, but no one suggested not going public. Just as well, Jack thought. He didn't want to have to remind them of their legal or fiduciary responsibilities.

"You asked me if I knew about this," he said. "What about all of you?"

Baynes looked at him. "What are you suggesting?"

"That you were his board. Many of you had known my father for years. He would have talked to you."

Baynes shook his head. "George didn't confide in anyone. This was his company. He made that clear before he went public. Things would be done his way."

"So you just let him run the company into the ground?"

The woman, Mrs. Keen, leaned forward. "George presented us with financial reports. We had no reason to doubt their validity or his. Your father wasn't a bad man, Jack, but clearly he was in over his head."

That seemed to be the consensus, he thought. "Shouldn't you, as his board, have noticed that? Shouldn't you have made sure the man running Hanson Media Group knew what he was doing?"

"Attacking us isn't going to solve the problem," Baynes said firmly.

Right. Because they were all more concerned about covering their collective asses, Jack thought grimly.

"We need to present a united front," Mrs. Keen said. "Perhaps the board should issue a statement as well."

"Do what you'd like," Jack told her.

"Things would go better if we could announce that you would be taking on your father's job permanently," Baynes said.

Jack narrowed his gaze. "I agreed to three months and that's all. I'm not changing my mind."

"Be reasonable," the older man said. "This is a crisis. The company is in real danger. We have employees, stockholders. We have a responsibility to them."

"No, *you* have one."

"You're George Hanson's oldest son," Mrs. Keen said. "People will look to you for leadership."

"I'm not his only son," he pointed out. "I have two brothers."

Baynes dismissed them with a wave of his hand. "Who are where? They don't have the experience, the education or the temperament for this kind of work."

Jack did his best not to lash out at them. Losing his temper would accomplish nothing. "Three months," he said. "That's all. In the meantime, I suggest you start looking for an interim president. Hire someone who knows what he or she is doing."

"But—"

Jack stood. "There's no point in having a conversation about me staying or going. I'm not changing my mind. Besides, we don't even know who owns the majority of the company. My father's shares are in limbo until the reading of the will. Who knows—maybe he'll want them sold on the open market."

The board members paled at the thought.

While they were still taking that in, he made his escape. As he walked down the hall, he loosened his tie. But that wasn't enough to wipe away the sense of being trapped.

"Come on, come on," Samantha called as she stared at the basket and willed the ball to slide cleanly through the hoop. There was a moment of silence, followed by a *swish* of net.

"Woo hoo." She held up her hand to Patti, one of her directors. "Two more for our team. We're up by six."

Patti gave her a high five, then went back into position. Perhaps playing basketball in the corridor right outside her office wasn't standard corporate procedure, but Samantha found it really helped her people clear their heads after a long day of brainstorming.

"Lucky shot," Phil said as he dribbled the ball. He jogged in to take his shot. Samantha moved in front of him. When he stretched up to shoot, she batted the ball away and it bounced off the wall before rolling down the hall.

The game went quiet as Jack rounded the corner and picked up the ball. Samantha could feel her staff looking at her. She knew Jack had endured the meeting from hell with the board and braced herself for him to take that out on her.

He raised his eyebrows. "Who's winning?"

"My team," she said quickly. "We've been brainstorming all day and we're—"

"No need to explain," he said, then bounced the ball. "Got room for one more?"

She glanced at Phil, who shrugged. "Sure," she said.

Jack tossed the ball back, then took off his jacket. After pulling off his tie, he went to work on rolling up his sleeves.

"Who's on the other team?" he asked.

"I am," Phil said, then he quickly introduced everyone else. "Any good at this?"

Jack grinned. "Just get me the ball."

Ten minutes later, Samantha knew they'd been had. Jack wasn't just good—he was terrific. He could shoot from any angle and he rarely missed. His team pulled ahead and then beat hers by six points.

"You're a ringer," she said, trying to catch her breath.

"I've had some practice."

"Where'd you play?" Phil asked, after slapping him on the back.

"Law school. We all did, to unwind. Grad school, too, but not so much."

Samantha remembered that Jack had attended law school before going to Wharton. She also vaguely recalled him hanging out with friends on the basketball courts, but she'd never paid much attention.

Now she knew she'd made the right decision. Being close to Jack while he ran, dodged, threw and scored bordered on dangerous. She liked the way his body moved and the energy he put in the game. She liked how he worked with his team and how, when his shirt came unbuttoned, she got a glimpse of some very impressive abs.

Bad idea, she reminded herself. Lusting after the boss could only lead to trouble. Okay, so she wasn't ready for a real relationship—maybe it was time to find rebound guy.

"Thanks for letting me play," Jack told Phil.

"Any time."

"There's that pub on the corner," Jack continued. "Why don't I buy you all drinks." He glanced at his watch. "Say half an hour?"

"Great." Phil grinned. "Thanks."

"No problem."

Samantha waited until everyone else had disappeared into their respective offices. "You didn't have to do that."

"Buy them drinks?" He shrugged. "I wanted to. They let me play. I needed the break."

"The board meeting?"

"Yeah." He shrugged into his jacket. "You're coming, aren't you?"

She shouldn't. It wasn't smart. It wasn't a lot of things. "Sure. I'll be there."

"Good."

He smiled and her toes curled. She walked into her office. Rebound guy—absolutely. She would have to get right on that.

Jack didn't just order drinks, he ordered platters of appetizers, then proceeded to talk to each member of her team individually. Samantha watched him work the crowd and did her best not to react when he smiled at one of her female staffers.

Finally he settled in the stool next to hers. "You've done well," he said in a low voice. "You have good people working for you."

"Thanks."

Despite the easy conversation around them, she was aware of being watched. Some of her team were mildly interested while a few—the single women—were trying to figure out the score.

"How did it go?" she asked.

"About as expected. They're more interested in protecting themselves than what really happened. We're making an announcement first thing in the morning. I have two phone calls scheduled with investors. The first is to tell them what happened, the second will come later when I announce our specific plan to rectify the situation."

"Do you have a plan?"

He sipped his drink. "Not yet, but I'm hopeful." He glanced around. "They're all working their butts off. I want to make sure it's not for nothing."

"It won't be. There will be some bad press, but we'll get through it."

"Until the next crisis."

"The company is in transition," she said. "There are always adjustments."

"I know. What I don't understand is why my father never had a successor picked out. He had to know he wasn't going to live forever."

"Maybe he was waiting for one of his sons to get interested in the company."

Jack took another drink. "Probably. I don't see Evan and Andrew making a beeline to Chicago and, honestly, I can't see either of them being willing to take things over."

She touched his arm. "You don't have to do this if you don't want to."

"I'm aware I can walk away at any point."

But he wouldn't. Jack had a sense of responsibility. She respected that about him.

Once again her body reminded her that he was nothing like Vance, but her head wasn't so sure. On the surface her ex had been a great guy, too. Successful, a caring father. He'd said and done all the right things—right up until the wedding. Then overnight he'd changed.

Her father had done the same thing. In a

matter of weeks, he'd gone from a loving, supportive man to someone who'd walked out and had done his best not to have to support his only child.

Powerful men often hid dark, guilty secrets. As much as she was attracted to Jack, she was determined to keep their relationship strictly professional. She couldn't afford to take another emotional hit right now.

"I should go," she said, collecting her purse.

"I'm heading out, too," he told her. "Want a ride home?"

Ah, the close confines of a car. So tempting and so dangerous.

"No, thanks. I have a few errands to run on my way home. I'll walk."

"Are you sure? I don't mind."

She smiled. "I appreciate the offer, but I'll be fine on my own."

She'd learned it was the only safe way to be.

Chapter Five

Roger Arnet was a tall, thin blond man in his mid-fifties. He shook Jack's hand, then sat in the visitor's chair on the other side of the desk.

"How are you settling in?" Roger asked pleasantly. "Your father was a great man. A great man. You won't find filling his shoes easy."

Jack didn't know how to answer the question. News of the second set of books had been released to the public. The response in the press had been relatively mild since Hanson Media Group wasn't a major player in the city, but there had been plenty of uproar in the office. He wondered if Roger had any way of reconciling his insistence that George had been a great man with the reality of a company president who lied to his entire staff.

"I'm finding my way," he said, going for a neutral response.

"Good. Good." Roger smiled. "I understand you're a lawyer."

"Yes. I attended law school, then went on to business school. It was my deal with my father. I would study both and then pick."

"You chose the law. George was very disappointed."

Had his father spoken about him with everyone in the firm? "I'm here now," Jack said. "Which is why I wanted to talk with you. We're making some changes."

"I heard about them," Roger said. "I've been on vacation and when I got back, everyone was buzzing. The Internet, eh? Are you sure about that?"

"Very sure."

Roger took off his glasses and pulled out a handkerchief. "Arnie's been filling me in on your plans. Very ambitious. Very ambitious. A bit too much, if you ask me."

Jack leaned back in his chair. "Are you saying we're not capable of expanding our Web sites?"

"Expansion is one thing, but what you're proposing is something else. But then it's not you, is it? It's that new girl. Samantha something."

"Edwards. And she has my full support."

"Of course. She's very energetic, but in my experience, it's better if we take things slowly. Sort of feel our way. Technology is all fine and good, but this company was founded on print media."

"Magazines are expensive and change slowly," Jack said. "We don't have any publication that has circulation over a million. We're barely breaking even on thirty percent of our magazines and we're losing money on the rest.

The Internet is a significant part of our culture. It's not going away. Changes can be made there relatively inexpensively."

Roger nodded. Jack felt as if he'd just stepped into an alternative universe. If Roger was the head of IT in the company, shouldn't he be pushing for *more* technology, not less?

"Arnie mentioned all of this to me," Roger admitted. "But he's young and he tends to get ahead of himself. I hope he wasn't filling your head with a lot of nonsense."

Jack was willing to respect those older than him and he was certainly willing to listen to qualified opinions; however, he wasn't willing to be treated like an idiot.

He straightened and stared directly at Roger. "Let me be as clear as possible," he said. "This company is on the brink of financial ruin. I'm sure you've read about our recent problems. The announcement that my father kept a second set of books wasn't happy news. Doing business the old way isn't going to keep this company going. We need change and we need it quickly. I believe that technology is our best solution. Now you can get onboard with that program or you can find another company that is more to your liking."

Roger blinked. "That's very blunt."

"Yes, it is. I've heard good things about you and I hope you'll decide to stay, but if you do, be aware that we have a new direction and I expect everyone to be excited about it."

"All right. I'll consider what you said. As far as the Internet expansion, I'm concerned about the safeguards. Your target market is children and there are many predators out there."

Jack wasn't sure how to read him. Still, the truth would come out quickly enough. Either Roger was with him or Roger was gone.

"Protecting the children using our site is our first priority," Jack told the other man.

"Samantha's first presentation was on Internet safeguards. She and Arnie are working very closely on that project. I appreciate your concern as well and I would ask you to oversee their work. Feel free to report back to me on any weak areas."

Roger seemed surprised. "Why should you trust me?"

"I believe you're genuinely concerned about the children," Jack said. "You're also slightly mistrustful of the changes. That will make you a good custodian of the security programs. You won't let anyone cut corners."

"Thank you for that. Let me think about all that you've said and get back to you."

"Of course. Thanks for coming in."

Roger shook hands with him, then walked to the door. Once there, he turned back. "I wish you could have seen your father at work here, Jack. He was brilliant. Simply brilliant."

"So I've heard."

* * *

Restless after his meeting with Roger, Jack headed to Samantha's office.

"Got a minute?" he asked as she hung up the phone.

"Sure. Have a seat."

He glanced at the light wood furniture, the bright prints on the walls and the purple sofa by the corner. In a matter of a week or two, Samantha had taken the space and made it her own.

"Interesting decorating," he said as he settled in a chair.

She grinned. "You hate it."

"Hate is strong."

"There's a lot of really cool stuff in the company storage facility."

"Some of it dating back to the sixties," Jack murmured.

"You're right. I didn't want to get too wild, but I like having color to inspire me."

Which, apparently, applied to her clothes, he

thought as he took in the orange-and-gold tunic top she'd pulled on over black slacks. Her hair was loose, in a riot of red curls that tangled in her beaded dream weaver earrings.

By contrast, his suit that day was gray, his shirt white and his tie a traditional burgundy. They couldn't be more different. Which is what had always made their relationship interesting, he reminded himself.

"What's up?" she asked.

"Have you met Roger Arnet?"

She wrinkled her nose. "Arnie's boss, right? I shook hands with him in passing, but we haven't spoken."

"Be prepared. He's not one to move with the times. He's opposed to the Internet expansion on many levels. He thinks the plans are too ambitious."

"Great. Just what I need. The person in charge of a critical department for me not getting onboard."

"I know he's going to be a problem. I told him he could get with the program or get out."

Her eyes widened. "That's not subtle."

"It's my style. I think he's a little more willing to compromise now. He does have one legitimate concern and that's to keep the site secure. Children are vulnerable."

"I agree and I've been working with the IT guys on different ideas for that. We're going cutting edge. No stalkers allowed."

"Roger felt very passionately about it, as well. You might want to put him on the team."

Samantha recoiled physically. "Do I have to?"

She sounded more like a twelve-year-old than a responsible adult.

"No, you don't," he said, holding in a smile. "It's your show. You can do what you like. I'm simply pointing out that sometimes it's better to find a way to work with those who don't agree with us. If you make Roger feel important and really use him on the project, you're more likely to win him over. I'll fire him if I have to, but I would prefer not to. He knows the company and he knows his job. All my reports about him are excellent."

"Good point," she murmured. "I'll do the mature thing and work with him. But I won't like it."

"No one is asking you to."

"Good to know."

She stood up and walked to a coffeepot on a low table by the window. When she held it out to him, he nodded. She poured two cups.

He took the one she offered and watched her walk back to her seat. He liked the way she moved and the way her clothes swayed with each step. When she sat back down, she sniffed her coffee before sipping, as if making sure no one had accidentally changed her drink for something else.

She'd been doing that for as long as he could remember. He used to tease her about it, which always sparked a furious argument during which she denied the action. Then he would hand her coffee and she would sniff and they would both laugh.

But this time he didn't say anything. A couple of nights ago, at the pub, she'd shut him down good. She'd been doing it in various ways ever since they'd first met. At some point he was going to have to accept the truth. Samantha simply didn't want him.

In his world, chemistry usually went both ways, but she was the exception to the rule. No matter how powerful the need inside of him, she didn't feel it. It was time to accept that and move on.

"Nothing about this job is boring," she said. "You have to admit that."

"Right now I'd be happy with a few days of boring. That would mean no new crisis."

She sighed. "You've been going from one to the other. That can't be easy."

He shrugged. "It is what it is. I'll deal with it. Are you still enjoying your condo?"

"Very much. You were right—the location is fabulous. Have you had pizza from that place across the street?"

"I'm a regular."

She sipped her coffee, then sighed. "I ordered it the other night. It's amazing. It was so good, I actually had some for breakfast. I've never done that in my life—not even in college. Until I tasted their pizza, I never really understood the whole deep-dish thing. But now I get it. Heaven. Pure heaven."

"Wait until you order their pasta."

"Really? I might do that tonight. I'm hoping to get out this weekend and explore a little more of the neighborhood. So far all I've seen is work and my building."

He consciously had to keep from offering to be her guide. He generally spent Saturday mornings with Charlie in the park, but a walking tour would give his dog plenty of exercise. They could—

No, he told himself. Samantha had made her position incredibly clear. He wasn't going to push anymore.

"You can go online," he said. "There's lots of information about the city there. Points of interest, planned walks, that sort of thing."

"Thanks," she said, sounding a little puzzled. "I'll do that. But if you're not busy we could—"

Mrs. Wycliff knocked on the open door. "Mr. Hanson, you have a call from Mr. Baynes."

He rose. "I need to take that," he told her, aware she'd been about to suggest something for the weekend. While he wanted to accept and spend more time with her, he knew it would be a mistake. He'd spent too much time wanting what he couldn't have where Samantha was concerned. He needed to move on.

Saturday, Samantha dressed for the cool, clear weather, then collected what she would need for a morning spent exploring. As she stepped out of her condo, she thought about going up to Jack's place and asking him to join her. Except she had a feeling he would say no.

Not that she could blame him. She'd been so careful to shut him down time and time again, shouldn't she be happy that he finally got the message? It was better for both of them if they were simply work colleagues.

She walked to the elevator and hit the down button. It was better, she told herself. Sure Jack was a great guy, but he was also the type of man to push all of her buttons and not in a good way. As much as she liked him, she was also wary of him. He was too much like her father and Vance. Too much in charge. She'd been fooled already—she wasn't willing to go there again.

Not that she was even looking for a serious relationship, she reminded herself. The best thing would be to find rebound guy and make that work. If only Jack weren't so sexy and smart and fun to be with.

She stepped out into the crisp morning and drew in a deep breath. Enough, she thought. For the rest of the day, she refused to think about Jack. She would simply enjoy herself and—

Something bumped into the back of her legs. She turned and saw Charlie. The border collie gave her a doggy grin, then barked. Jack smiled.

"Morning," he said, looking delicious in worn jeans and a sweatshirt.

"Hi."

"Out to see the sights?"

She tugged on the strap of her purse/backpack. "I have everything I need right here. Maps, water, money for a cab in case I get lost."

"You picked a good day. It won't get too hot."

Was it just her, or had things taken a turn for

the awkward? "So you and Charlie are headed for the park?"

He nodded. "Every Saturday, regardless of the weather."

She rubbed the dog's ears. The smart choice was simply to walk away. But she was lonely, she liked Jack and she wanted them to be friends.

"Can a non-dog owner come along?" she asked.

He hesitated, but before she could retract the question, he smiled. "Sure. When I get tired of throwing Charlie the Frisbee, you can take over."

"I'd like that." She fell into step beside him. "So how did you get Charlie? Did you grow up with dogs in the house?"

"No. I wasn't actually looking for a pet. Then a buddy from my law firm invited me over for dinner. I learned later it was with an ulterior motive. His dog had six-week-old puppies he was looking to sell to unsuspecting friends. Charlie and I bonded over a game of tag."

She laughed. "I wouldn't have thought a hotshot-attorney type could be influenced so easily."

"Don't tell anyone. He moved in a couple of weeks later and I quickly found out that puppies are a ton of work. For a year he chewed everything he could get his teeth on. Then I took him to obedience training and now we understand each other better."

They stopped at the red light on the corner. Charlie waited patiently until the light changed, then led them along the crosswalk.

"Have you been reading the papers?" Jack asked.

She had a feeling he didn't mean the fashion reports. "I've noticed there was some local coverage on Hanson Media Group, but I could only find a couple of articles in the national papers. You're right—there wasn't all that much press."

"Sometimes it's good to be small, relatively

speaking. Now if we were one of the networks, it would be a different story."

"I'm surprised no one ever made any offer to buy the company out," she said. "So much of entertainment is now controlled by conglomerates."

"For all I know my father's been fighting off offers for years. He wouldn't sell and risk losing his name on the letterhead."

He sounded bitter as he spoke. "You don't agree?" she asked.

"It's not my thing. I don't need to be the center of the universe, at least as my father defined it."

They'd reached the park.

"The dog zone is on the other side," he said. "Hope you don't mind the hike."

"Exercise is my friend," she said with a grin. "At least that's what I tell myself."

"There's a gym in the building."

"They showed it to me on my tour. Very impressive." There had been several treadmills and ellipticals, along with weight machines and three sets of free weights.

"I work out every morning," Jack said. "It's pretty quiet at five."

"In the morning?" She shuddered. "That's because more normal people are sleeping. I can't believe you get up that early."

"I'm lucky. I don't need a lot of sleep."

"Apparently not. Most of the year, it's dark at that time."

"They have lights in the gym."

They'd need more than that to get her there. Coffee, for starters. And bagels.

"I'm not really into the whole sweat thing," Samantha told him. "I've been lucky. I don't seem to gain weight."

It sort of went with what was kindly referred to as a boyish figure. She decided it was a trade-off. Sure she didn't have anything to fill out her bras and padding was required to hint at anything resembling cleavage, but she'd never counted calories or given up carbs. She could eat what she wanted and still have the world's boniest butt.

"Exercise isn't just about weight loss. It keeps you healthy."

"So does getting enough sleep. Besides, I'm a big walker. I can go for miles." As long as there was plenty of food along the way. One of the things she missed about New York. All the street vendors and little delis where a pretzel or ice-cream craving could be instantly satisfied.

They walked through a grove of trees and came out in a huge open area. There were already a half-dozen dog owners and their pets running around. Jack found a spot in the sun and set down his backpack.

"Equipment," she said. "So what exactly is involved in your Saturday-morning ritual?"

He pulled out a blanket. "For me," he said. Then a ball. "For Charlie. We start with this and work up to the Frisbee."

He unclipped Charlie from the leash, then threw the red rubber ball what seemed like at least a quarter mile.

Charlie took off after it, grabbed it and raced toward him.

"Impressive," she said. "The dogs don't get crabby with each other?"

"Not usually. Most people know if their dogs are social or not. There have been the occasional fights, but it's rare."

Charlie bounded toward them and dropped the ball at her feet. She winced.

"I throw like a girl," she told the dog. "You won't be impressed."

Jack laughed. "Come on. He's not going to be critical."

"Uh-huh. You say that now, but neither of you has seen me throw."

She picked up the slightly slobbery ball, braced herself and threw as hard as she could. It made it, oh, maybe a third of the way it had before. Charlie shot her a look that clearly asked if that was the best she could do before running after the ball. This time when he returned, he dropped it at Jack's feet.

"So much for not being critical," she said.

Jack laughed and tossed the ball again.

They settled on the blanket. The sun felt good in the cool morning. She could hear laughter and dogs barking. Families with children in strollers walked on the paved path that went around the dog park. There was the occasional canine tussle, but as Jack had said, no real trouble.

After about fifteen minutes of catch, Charlie came back and flopped down next to them.

"He's just resting," Jack told her. "Soon he'll be ready for the Frisbee. Then watch out. He can catch just about anything."

She rubbed the dog's belly. "I can't wait to see him in action."

"He'll show off for you."

"I hope so."

Charlie licked her arm, then closed his eyes and wiggled in the sun.

"What a life," she said. "I used to see dogs in New York all the time. I wondered what it was like for them to be in a city, but Charlie is hardly suffering."

Jack narrowed his gaze. "Is that a crack about the doggy day care?"

"No. Of course not. Why would I say anything about that?" She was careful not to smile as she spoke.

"Somehow I don't believe you, so I'm going to change the subject. Do you miss New York?"

She crossed her legs and shrugged out of her jacket. "Sure. It's a great city. But I can already see the potential here. The feeling is different, but in a good way. In New York I always felt I had to be going or doing or I'd miss something. I don't feel so frantic here."

"I like it. And the people. Are you missing your ex?"

A subtle way to ask about her divorce, she thought. It was a fair question. "No. The marriage was over long before I left. Unfortunately, I didn't notice."

"Did he agree with that?"

"No. Vance wasn't happy about me leaving." She ignored the memories of fights and screaming. "I just couldn't trust him anymore and once trust is destroyed, it's over."

"He cheated?"

The question surprised her until she realized it was a logical assumption, based on what she'd said. "Nothing that simple. I met Vance through my work—a fund-raiser I worked on. He's a cardiologist. He has an excellent reputation and everyone who knew us both thought we'd make a great couple. So did I. He was divorced, but was still really close with his kids. I thought that meant something."

Jack frowned. "You wanted kids."

"I'm surprised you remembered."

"You used to talk about it."

She laughed. "Right. You thought two was plenty. I wanted four. You were uncomfortable with three because an odd number would make travel difficult. Ever practical."

"It's true. Try finding a hotel room that sleeps five."

"Okay. Good point. Anyway Vance knew I wanted children. We discussed it at length." That's what got her, she thought. That he'd agreed. "We even discussed names."

"He changed his mind?"

"More than that. He lied." She shook her head. "I was such a fool. We decided to wait a little, get settled in our marriage. Then, when I was ready to start trying, he kept putting it off. I never suspected anything. Finally I pressured him into agreeing it was time."

She paused as she mentally edited her past. There were so many other reasons she'd left Vance, but this was the easiest to explain.

"Nothing happened," she said. "Months went by. Finally, I spoke to my doctor, who agreed to do some tests. It made sense for me to go in first. After all, Vance had already fathered children. I came through fine and then it was time for Vance to make an appointment. Only he wouldn't. He finally came clean. He'd had a vasectomy after his youngest was born. He'd been lying the whole time."

Jack hadn't known where the story was going, but he sure as hell hadn't guessed the ending. "Samantha, I'm sorry."

"Me, too." She ducked her head and rubbed Charlie's chest. "I was so angry, but more than that, I was hurt. I couldn't understand why he hadn't told me the truth when we'd first started dating. It would have been so easy. He lied. Worse than that, he let me believe there was something wrong with me. He even hinted at it by telling me his first wife hadn't had any trouble getting pregnant."

He heard the betrayal in her voice and didn't know what to say. The man's actions made no sense. Why lie about something that was going to come out eventually? Why marry Samantha knowing she wanted kids and he didn't?

"What did he say?" he asked.

"Not much. That's what got me. He never took responsibility for his actions. He never thought he was wrong." She pulled her knees to her chest and wrapped her arms around her legs. "I can't tell you how much it hurt to find out the truth. It was as if I'd never known him. I thought he was different. I thought he was special, but I was wrong."

There was still pain in her eyes. Jack didn't know how long it would take to get over something like that. He knew a little of her past— that her father had walked out with no warning and had abandoned her and her mother. No wonder she was wary around men.

"Okay, this is boring," she said, a smile trembling on her lips. "Let's talk about something a little more perky. Like you. A lawyer, huh? Who would have thought."

"That's me—a man interested in the law."

"Really? But it's so stodgy."

He grinned. "Not to me."

"I don't know. All those thick books you have to read. Case law. So not my thing."

"Not to mention the clothes."

"Yeah. The dark suits would really depress me. So what's the game plan? You work your way up to senior partner, then torture new associates for sport?"

"That's one possibility."

"And the other?"

He didn't usually talk about his future plans with many people. Not that he didn't trust Samantha. "I want to be a judge."

She stretched her legs out in front of her. "Wow—that's pretty cool." She tilted her head and studied him. "I think you'd be good at it.

You're very calm and you reason things through. If only the robe weren't black."

He chuckled. "Every career has drawbacks."

"True, and that's not a big one. Judge Hanson. I like it. All the more reason to get back to your law firm."

"Exactly."

"Which means every disaster is something you can almost take personally," she murmured. "That's got to be hard on you."

He wasn't surprised that she understood. He and Samantha had never had a communication problem. Their friendship had been based on long nights spent talking, arguing and seeking common ground.

"I've agreed to stay for three months," he said. "When that time is up, I'm going back to my real job."

"The company won't be the same without you," she told him. "But I understand why you want to leave."

Charlie stretched, then stood and looked meaningfully at the backpack. Jack pulled out the Frisbee and threw it. Charlie raced after it and caught it in midair. Samantha scrambled to her feet.

"Did you see that? He's incredible. Does he always catch it?"

"Most of the time. Border collies are athletic dogs."

"I guess."

Charlie trotted the Frisbee back and put it at Jack's feet. Jack threw it farther this time.

"Amazing," Samantha said. "What a fun way to spend your Saturday morning. Do you always come to this park?"

"Mostly. There are a few other dog parks around the city. Sometimes we jog along the lake. You'll have fun exploring."

"I know," she said absently, watching his dog. "Although my travels will be limited by my lack of driving."

"What? You don't drive?"

She crossed her arms over her chest. "No, I don't. I never learned before I went to college and once there, I didn't have the opportunity. Since then I've been living in Manhattan. I did fine with public transportation or walking."

"You don't drive?" He couldn't imagine it. How could someone not know how to drive?

"No matter how many times you repeat the question, the answer's going to stay the same," she said. "It's not that big a deal."

"It's a little scary," he said. "Want me to teach you?"

The invitation came out before he could stop it. Instantly he braced himself for her standard refusal. What was wrong with him? Why couldn't he accept the fact that Samantha just wasn't into him that way?

"I've seen your fancy car," she said. "Too much pressure."

Was that a yes? Did he want it to be? Wasn't he done trying to make points with her?

"I can get my hands on an old clunker."

"Really? I'm tempted. I've always felt, I don't know, weird about the whole driving thing." She studied him. "You wouldn't yell, would you?"

"Not my style."

Charlie barked, urging the Frisbee game to continue. Jack ignored him.

"Then thank you for asking," she said. "I'd be delighted to take you up on your offer. But if you change your mind, you have to tell me. I don't want you doing something you don't want to do."

"Again, not my style."

She laughed. "Jack, you're currently doing a job you hate because it's the right thing to do."

He chuckled, realizing she had a point. "Not counting that."

Charlie barked again. Then he picked up the Frisbee he'd dropped and brought it to them.

Jack reached for it, as did Samantha. Their arms bumped, their shoulders crashed and the two of them tumbled onto the blanket.

Jack twisted and put out his hands to pull her against him, so he could take the weight of the fall. They landed with a thud that pushed out most of his air.

Her hands were on the blanket, her body pressed intimately against his. His legs had fallen apart and she lay nestled between his thighs. He could feel her breasts pressing against his chest.

Their eyes locked. Something darkened hers and all he could think about was kissing her.

There were a lot of reasons not to and only one reason he should.

Because he wanted to.

Chapter Six

Samantha felt the light brush of his mouth on hers. She knew she could easily stop him by saying something or simply rolling off him. It was the sensible thing to do. And yet she found herself not wanting to move. Her recollection of her previous kisses with Jack, from that one extraordinary night they'd shared, were still vivid in her mind. She was confident that she'd inflated their impressiveness over time. A kiss now would allow for comparison.

When she didn't move, he cupped her face

with his hands and angled his head. Then he kissed her again, this time moving his lips back and forth. She felt heat and soft pressure. Blood surged in her body, making her want to squirm closer. She was already right on top of him, their bodies touching in so many interesting places, but suddenly that wasn't enough. She needed more.

He moved his hands, easing them past her ears so he could bury his fingers in her hair. Then he parted his mouth and bit down on her bottom lip.

The unexpected assault made her breath catch. He took advantage of her parted lips and slipped his tongue inside.

It was like drowning in warm, liquid desire. Wanting crashed over her, filling every cell until it was all she could think of. His fingers still tangled in her hair, which made her impatient. She wanted him touching her…everywhere.

Even as he circled her tongue with his, teasing, tasting, arousing, her body melted. She felt herself softening, yielding, kissing him back with a desperation that made her the aggressor.

She took control of the kiss, following him back into his mouth, claiming him with quick thrusts of her tongue. At last he moved his hands to her back where he stroked the length of her spine. Her hips arched in an involuntary invitation, which brought her stomach in contact with something hard, thick and very masculine.

Memories crashed in on her. She remembered how he'd touched her and tasted her everywhere. She recalled the sight of him naked, of how many times he'd claimed her. She'd been sore for nearly two days, but the soreness had only reminded her of the incredible pleasure they'd shared and had made her want to do it again. But she'd resisted— because of who he was and what he could do to her heart.

She hated the logic filling her brain, the voice

that asked what was different now. She wasn't interested in danger or reality or anything but the way their bodies fit together. If she—

But an insistent barking distracted her and at last she lifted her head only to find Charlie's nose inches from her face.

Below her, Jack groaned. "I'm going to have to have a talk with that dog."

She became aware of their intimate position and the very public location. Without saying anything, she slid off him, then scrambled to her feet.

"We're in the park," she said more to herself than him. "In public."

Jack rose more slowly. He reached down for the Frisbee and tossed it, all without looking away from her.

"I doubt anyone noticed," he told her.

"Still." She pressed her hands to her heated face. Talk about acting out of character. She had always been a strictly-in-bed, lights-off kind of date. The only exception to that rule…was standing right next to her.

Of course. She was fine as long as she resisted Jack's particular brand of temptation, but if she gave in, even for a second, she completely lost her head.

"I, ah…" She glanced around, then returned her attention to him. "I'm, um, going to let you get back to your morning."

His dark eyes glowed with passion. "You don't have to."

"It's for the best."

His mouth straightened. "Let me guess. This was a mistake."

His tone of resignation caught her more than his words. He expected her to pull back because that's what she always did. There were several good reasons, but he didn't know them. If she had her way, he never would.

"Thanks for everything," she said, trying to smile. "I'll see you Monday."

She hesitated, then walked away when he didn't speak. A slight feeling of hurt surprised her. What did she expect? That he would come after her? Not likely after all the times she'd turned him down.

Jack watched her go. Once again Samantha was the queen of mixed signals. She had been from the beginning. Is that what made him want her? He never knew where he stood?

"Not exactly the basis of a great relationship," he murmured, throwing the Frisbee again.

The good news was Samantha wanted him sexually. The truth had been there in her response. For some reason, she couldn't handle the idea of it, but at least she didn't find him repulsive.

Was it him in particular or would she have run from anyone?

But she still liked to run and a guy with a brain in his head would let her go. Funny how he'd always been smart, everywhere in his life but with her. What was it about her that made him want to keep trying? It wasn't that he thought that they were soul mates. He didn't believe in that sort of thing and he sure as hell wasn't interested in a serious relationship. What was the point?

He was in it for the sex. Not a one-night stand. That wasn't fun anymore. He liked to take a lover for a few months, make sure they were both completely satisfied, then move on when one or both of them got restless.

Somehow he doubted Samantha would be up for anything like that.

Which left him where? Wanting a woman who didn't want him? There was a way to start the weekend. Okay, he was back to his original plan—forgetting about her as anything other than an employee.

Easier said than done, he thought as he remembered the feel of her body on his. But not impossible.

* * *

Jack reached for his coffee and cursed whoever had invented speakerphones and tele-conferences. Spending an hour explaining to stock analysts and trade journalists how he had found a second set of books was not his idea of a good time.

"You're sure the investigation into how this happened has already begun?" a disembodied voice asked.

"Of course. It started less than twelve hours after I found the books. It would have started sooner, but I couldn't get an independent accounting team in here until morning."

"You're not using your regular accountants, are you?"

"No. No one who has ever been associated with Hanson Media Group is involved. As soon as we have a preliminary report, I'll make it public. Until then, I don't have any answers."

"Do you think more people were involved than your father?"

Jack hesitated. "I don't have any specifics on that, but my personal opinion in that my father acted alone."

"Has his death been investigated? Are the company's troubles the reason he died?"

The not-so-subtle implication that George Hanson had killed himself infuriated Jack. He spoke through gritted teeth. "My father died of natural causes. There was an autopsy. He didn't kill himself." And he would sue any bastard who reported otherwise, Jack thought. He might not have been close to the old man, but he wouldn't let any member of his family be dragged through the press that way.

"Is the company going to make it?" someone asked.

Jack stared at the phone. In truth, he didn't have a clue. He continued to ride the bad-news train, with a new crisis every day. From where he sat, he couldn't imagine how this could be pulled off. In his opinion, it would take a miracle or a buyout for Hanson Media Group to survive, but he wasn't about to tell them that.

"We're going to come through this just fine," he said, wondering if saying it would make it reality.

Samantha had spent much of the weekend giving herself a stern talking-to. Being afraid was one thing, but acting like an idiot was another. She had to pick a side—any side. Either she was interested in Jack romantically or she wasn't.

She hated the mixed messages she sent every time they hung out together. She didn't like that she had become that sort of woman. In truth, she found him sexy and funny and smart and pretty much everything any reasonable single female would want in a man. But he was also rich, powerful, determined and used to getting his way, which terrified her.

There were actually two different problems. First, that however much she told herself she *wasn't* interested, that she only wanted a platonic relationship with him, her body had other plans. No matter how much her head held back, the rest of her was eager to plunge in the deep end and just go for it. The attraction was powerful and ten years after she'd first felt it, it didn't seem to be going away.

The second problem was also a head-body issue. However much her head could intellectualize that Jack was nothing like Vance or her father, her heart didn't believe. So she got close, he made a move, she reacted, then the fear kicked in and she bolted. It was a horrible pattern and short of never seeing him again in any capacity, she didn't know how to break it.

Whoever said acknowledging the problem was half the battle had obviously never lived in the real world. Understanding what was wrong didn't seem to move her any closer to solving it.

But solution or not, she owed Jack an apology and she was going to deliver it right now. Or in the next few minutes, she thought as she paced in front of his office. Mrs. Wycliff glanced at her curiously, but didn't say anything. Finally Samantha gathered her courage and walked purposefully toward the door. She knocked once and entered, careful to close the door behind herself. She didn't need any witnesses for her potential humiliation.

"Hi, Jack," she began, before starting her prepared speech. "I wanted to stop by and—"

She came to a stop in the center of the room and stared at him.

He sat at the conference table, the speaker-phone in front of him, notes spread out. He looked as if he'd received horrible news.

She hurried to the table. "What happened? Are you all right?"

He shrugged. "I'm fine. I had the phone call with several investors and some people from the street. It didn't go well."

Of course. The problems with Hanson Media Group. As if he weren't dealing with enough from that, she was torturing him on weekends. How spiffy.

"I'm sorry," she said, sinking into the chair across from his. "I'm guessing they had a lot of questions."

"Oh, yeah. Plenty of suggestions, too. None of them especially helpful. But this is why they pay me the big bucks, right? So I can take the heat."

Maybe. But Jack wasn't interested in the money or the job. "Talk about a nightmare," she murmured.

"One I can't wake up from. But that's not why you stopped by. What's up?"

"I wanted to tell you I'm sorry about what happened on—"

"Stop," he said. "No apologizes required."

"But I want to explain. It's not what you think."

He raised his eyebrows.

She sighed. "Okay. Maybe it is what you think. I'm having some trouble making up my mind about what I want. I'm working on that. The thing is, I don't want you to think it's about you. It's not. It's about me, and well, who you are. Which isn't the same as it being about you."

He smiled. "None of that made sense, but it's okay. Let's just forget it and move on. You didn't like what happened and I'm okay with that."

She started to tell him that she *had* liked him kissing her, but stopped herself. That wasn't the point…at least she didn't think it was.

"You push my buttons," she admitted instead. "You have some qualities in common with my ex-husband."

Jack winced. "Not the good ones, right?"

"Sorry, no."

"Just my luck." He glanced out the window at the view of the city. Rain darkened the horizon and made the lights sparkle. "Life would be a lot less complicated without relationships."

"Not possible. Then we'd be nothing but robots."

"Or just very sensible people. Like Vulcans."

She smiled. "I'm not sure we should aspire to pointed ears."

"But their philosophy—no emotion. I understand the appeal."

"Too much pressure?" she asked, already knowing the answer.

"Too much everything. I remember when I was a lot younger. My brothers and I really got along. My father was busy with work, so there was just us and whatever nanny worked for him that month."

"I'm guessing the three of you were a handful."

He grinned. "Full of energy and imagination. It was an interesting combination. What I can't figure out is when we stopped being a family. That's David's big complaint and he's right. We don't pull together. I want to blame my father, but that only works so long. The three of us are grown-ups. We need a new excuse."

"Or maybe a way to change things. Would you like to be close to your brothers now?"

He nodded slowly. "Maybe together we could figure out how to fix this mess. But I can't get Evan and Andrew to return my calls. When it's time to read the will, I'll have to drag them back here. It's crazy."

"But they will come back," she said. "You could talk to them."

"I don't know what to say anymore. How sad is that?"

She had to agree it was pretty awful. If she had a brother or sister, she wouldn't ever want to lose touch.

"Maybe if you talk to Helen," she said without thinking. "She might have some ideas."

Jack looked at her. "No, thanks."

Samantha felt herself bristle. "What is it with you?" she asked. "Why won't you even give the woman a chance? Name me one thing she's done that you don't approve of. Give me one example of where she screwed up big time."

"I don't have any specific events," he said.

"Then what's the problem? You said you trusted my opinion of her and were going to stop assuming the worst." He made her crazy. Jack could be so reasonable about other things, but when it came to Helen, he refused to be the least bit logical.

"I don't think the worst," he said.

"You certainly don't think anything nice. She's pretty smart. Why don't you talk to her about the business?"

"My father wouldn't have told her anything."

"How do you know?"

"He didn't talk to anyone about the company."

"To the best of your knowledge. Did it ever

occur to you that he might have married her *because* she's smart and capable? That maybe when things went bad, he talked to her." She held up both hands. "I'm not saying I know anything. But neither do you. You treat Helen like she's a twenty-one-year-old bimbo your father married because she had big breasts. It's crazy. You have an asset there you're not using."

He looked at her. "You're a very loyal friend."

"Helen makes it easy to be. Will you at least think about what I've said?"

He nodded. "Promise."

She was fairly sure she believed him. Jack had never lied to her. But why was this an issue in the first place? Why didn't he already know his stepmother's good points? Every family had secrets, but this one seemed to have more than most.

"It was just my mom and me," she said. "I can't relate to problems inherent in a large family."

"Want to trade?" he asked, then grimaced.

"I'm sorry. I know you and your mom were close. You must still miss her."

She nodded, thinking she'd missed her most during the last few months of her marriage. When she'd wondered if Vance was really what she'd thought or if she'd been overreacting.

"We'd always had a special relationship," she said, "but we got even closer after my dad left. There was something about worrying about our next meal that put things in perspective."

"The man was a first-class bastard," Jack told her. "You haven't talked to him since?"

"He never wanted to talk to me. When I got older, I tried a few times, but eventually I gave up. He just wasn't interested. I heard he passed away a couple of years after my mom."

"I won't say I'm sorry. Not about him."

"I always think that things could have been different. I wasn't interested in him for what I could get. I just wanted a relationship with my father. But he never understood that. Why do relationships have to be so complicated?"

"Not a clue."

She stood. "Okay, I've taken up enough of your time. I just wanted to tell you that I'm sorry."

"Don't be."

"Thanks, Jack."

She left, not sure if she'd made things better or worse between them. She had a feeling that the only way to really solve the problem was to make a decision one way or the other and stick to it. If she was going to keep things business only, then she should not go to his office to chat. If she was interested in something else, then she should do that.

Complications, she thought. Questions and no answers. At least her life was never boring.

Jack returned from his working lunch meeting with the vice president of finance to find his stepmother waiting for him in his office.

Helen smiled when she saw him. "I was in the neighborhood," she said.

Under normal circumstances, he would have been polite and done his best to get her gone as quickly as possible. Since his last conversation with Samantha, he was curious to find out what Helen wanted.

He motioned to the leather sofa in the corner. Helen crossed the room and took a seat. He followed and settled in a club chair, then tried to figure out what was different about her today.

She was still pretty, blond and only a few years older than him. Not exactly a bimbo, as Samantha had pointed out, but still very much a trophy wife.

While she wasn't dressed in widow's black— did anyone still do that today?—she'd replaced her normally bright clothes with a navy tailored pantsuit. She'd pulled her hair back and, except for simple earrings and her wedding band, she seemed to have abandoned the heavy jewelry she usually favored.

"How are you doing?" he asked. "Is everything all right at the house?"

She frowned slightly. "I don't understand."

"You're alone in the house. I know it's large and I wondered if you were coping all right."

Eyebrows rose slowly. "You can't possibly be concerned about me."

He shrugged. "I'm asking."

"Hmm. All right. I'm doing fine. Yes, the house is big and empty, but your father worked long hours, so I'm used to being there alone."

Jack shifted in his seat and wished he'd never started the damn conversation in the first place. But he was already into it. "Are you, ah, sleeping?"

She sighed. "Not really. I still expect George to walk in and apologize for working late again. But he doesn't." She smiled. "Enough of my concerns. They're not why I stopped by. I wanted to check on you. It's been a difficult couple of weeks."

"You've been reading the paper."

"Several. There wasn't a lot of mention in the national press, which is something, but we're

getting plenty of local coverage. I feel just
horrible, Jack. I wish I could make this all better."

So did he. "Did you know about the second
set of books?"

He watched her as she spoke to see if she got
uncomfortable, but her cool gaze never flickered.

"I didn't. George didn't talk about the
business very much with me. I wanted him to.
I was interested. But he just wasn't one to do
that. I do know that for the last year or so
before he died that he was under a lot of stress.
I had an idea there were problems with the
company, but I had no idea they were this
bad."

He wanted to believe her. Right now he had
enough bad news without thinking there was
someone making trouble from the inside. Not
that Helen worked for the company, but until
the will was read, she controlled his father's
stock. Speaking of which…

"Do you know what's in his will?" he asked
bluntly.

"No. He never discussed that with me, either."

"So what did you talk about?"

"Everyday things." She crossed her legs. "Jack, I'm not the enemy here. I always thought things would be better if you, your father and your brothers could reconcile."

"How magnanimous of you."

She drew in a breath. "So you still don't like me."

"I don't know you. Why is that?"

"I don't know," she said, surprising him. "I wanted to get to know you and Evan and Andrew. I invited you all over several times. You were the only one to come."

Jack remembered the lone uncomfortable dinner he'd attended. His father had spent the entire time telling him that his decision to go into the law instead of joining Hanson Media Group was foolish at best. That no good would come of it. Jack recalled walking out sometime between the salad and main course.

"He wasn't an easy man," he said.

"I know, but for what it's worth, I don't think he meant to be so difficult. He tended to see things one way."

"His."

"He wanted you to be happy."

Jack grimaced. "He wanted me to run his company, regardless of what I wanted."

"Here you are," she said softly.

"Lucky me."

"I wish things were different," she said. "I wish he weren't dead. Not just for me, but for you. I wish you didn't have to do this."

"There isn't anyone else," he reminded her. "I'm stuck."

"You're the best choice. I'm sorry this is taking you away from what you love but the company is important, too. We all have to make sacrifices."

"Not from where I'm sitting. So far it's a sacrifice committee of one. I wish I knew what was in the will. Maybe he left everything to you and I can screw up enough that you'll fire me."

She shook her head. "Don't hold your breath on that one. George was always interested in surprising people. I doubt he wrote a boring will."

He believed that. "If he left the company to me, I'm selling."

She stiffened. "Just like that? Your father gave his life to this company."

"I know that better than anyone, except maybe you."

"I loved him, which means I can forgive his flaws."

The implication being Jack should do the same.

He wanted to ask her how that was possible. How could she give her heart to a man who made sure she always came in second. But he didn't. There wasn't any point. People who were supposed to love you left, one way or the other. Some disappeared into work or circumstances. Some walked away and some died. But at the end of the day, everyone was alone. He'd learned that a long time ago and he didn't plan to forget it.

Chapter Seven

Samantha was reasonably confident that driving lessons were a bad idea all around. For one thing, Jack should be really mad at her. For another, the situation had the potential to turn into a disaster.

"Second thoughts?" he asked from the passenger seat of the old import parked in an empty parking lot.

"Oh, I'm way past them. I'm on to deep regret and remorse."

"You'll be fine," he said. "It's easy. Think of all the crazy people you know who can drive."

"Telling me I'm likely to encounter the insane isn't a way to make me feel better," she told him. "Really. Let's talk about all the safe drivers instead."

"There are a lot of them. You'll be one of them. All you have to do is relax."

Oh, sure. Because that was going to happen. She peered out the windshield and was dismayed to note there wasn't a single cloud in the sky. Not even a hint of rain or bad weather or impending anything that would give her a good excuse to call off the session.

"You don't have to do this," she said. "I could hire someone."

"I don't mind. It will be fun."

Maybe for him. She curled her fingers around the steering wheel and sighed. "I don't think I'm up to it."

"Of course you are. You're afraid, which makes sense, but once you let go of the fear, you'll be fine. Think of the end goal. You'll be driving. You can go anywhere you want. You won't be dependent on bus schedules or trains. You're free. Close your eyes."

She looked at him. "I may not know much about driving but even I know that's a bad way to start."

He laughed. "You'll open them before we go anywhere. Close your eyes."

She did as he asked.

"Now imagine yourself driving on a big highway. The lanes are wide and it's divided so you don't have to worry about oncoming traffic. There are only a few cars and none of them are near you. It's a pretty day. You're going north, to Wisconsin. Can you imagine it?"

She did her best to see the road and not the flashing telephone poles or trees beckoning her to crash into them. She imagined herself driving easily, changing lanes, even passing someone.

"Now see yourself getting off the highway. At the top of the exit, you stop, then turn into a diner. You're completely comfortable. You're driving and it's easy."

She drew in a deep breath, then opened her eyes. "Okay. I'm ready."

"Good. We've been over the basics. Tell me what you remember."

She talked her way through starting the car, putting it in gear and checking her mirrors. Long before she wanted him to, he told her it was time to replace visualization with actual doing.

She started the engine. Of course it sprang to life. She carefully shifted into D and then checked her mirrors. They were blissfully alone in the parking lot.

"Here I go," she murmured as she took her foot off the brake and lightly pressed on the gas.

The car moved forward. It wasn't so bad. She'd had a couple of driving lessons back in college and she'd enjoyed those. These weren't all that different.

"Signal and turn right," Jack said.

Signal? She flipped on the indicator then turned. Unfortunately, she pulled the wheel too far and they went in a circle. Instantly she slammed on the brakes.

"Sorry."

"It's fine," he told her. "Don't worry about it. We're here to practice. If you could get it right the first time, why would you need to practice?"

He was being so logical and nice, she thought. Vance would have been screaming at her the whole time.

"Let's try that turn again," Jack said.

"Okay." She drove straight, put on her signal, then eased the car into a turn. It did as she asked.

"Wow. That was pretty easy."

"Told you," he said with a smile. "We'll make a couple more laps of the parking lot, then go onto the street."

"The street?" she asked, her voice a screech. From the back seat Charlie raised his head as if asking what was wrong.

"You can't stay in this parking lot forever," Jack said.

"Of course I can. It's a great parking lot. I like it. I could live here."

"You'll be fine. Come on. More driving. That way."

He pointed in front of them. She drove for another five minutes, making turns and coming to a stop when he told her. Despite her protests, he managed to convince her to head out onto the actual street.

"This is an industrial park," he said. "It's Saturday. There aren't going to be a lot of cars. Deep breaths."

She held in a small scream then took the plunge. Or, in this case, the driveway onto the street. Up ahead was an on-ramp to the highway and all the open road she could want. Like a cat let out of a carrier, she traded freedom for safety and took a side street. The highway would still be there tomorrow.

* * *

"And?" he asked as they cruised the produce section of the local market.

"You were great," she said. "Just terrific. Patient, calm and happy to explain everything fifty times."

He shook his head. "While I appreciate the compliments, they weren't the point. Admit it. The driving wasn't so bad."

It hadn't been. After nearly an hour in the industrial park, she'd actually driven back into the city. There had been a single harrowing experience at an intersection when some jerk had jumped the light and nearly hit her, but aside from that it had been…easy.

"You're a good teacher," she said.

"You're a good driver."

She sighed. "I am, aren't I? Soon I'll be really good. Then I'll have my license."

"Then you can buy a car."

"Oh. Wow." She'd never thought in actual

terms of getting a car. "I like it. There are so many kinds. I could get a little convertible."

"Not a great choice in winter."

"Hmm. You're right. But maybe something sporty. Or an SUV. Then I could haul stuff on weekends."

"Do you have anything to haul?"

"I don't think so. Is it required?"

"The dealer isn't going to ask."

"Okay. Or maybe I could get a hybrid. That's more environmentally friendly and I always recycle."

He looked at her as if she'd suddenly grown horns.

"What?" she asked.

"Nothing. You about ready?"

She eyed the strawberries, then nodded. "I'm always tempted by out-of-season fruit. It's a thing with me."

He pointed to her overflowing basket. "You know, this store delivers."

"I heard, but I like to buy my own groceries. Check stuff out. What if I change my mind about what I want for dinner?"

"What? You don't carefully plan a menu for the entire week and then stick with it?" he asked.

She felt her eyes widen a split second before she realized he was teasing her. "No, I don't. But you rigid types plan everything."

"I've had a few surprises lately."

She was sure he was talking about the company, but she suddenly wished he were talking about the kiss they'd shared. That had been…nice.

She'd enjoyed knowing that her nerve endings hadn't died in the divorce and that, yes, eventually she would want to be with another man. Although she had a feeling that her powerful sexual reaction had specifically been about Jack, there was still hope for her future. Eventually she would find someone else to be interested in.

They went through the checkout, then Jack

helped her load her bags of groceries into the trunk.

"Let's go," he said, opening the passenger door.

She stood on the sidewalk. "Wait. I can't drive back to our building."

"Why not? It's just around the corner."

"Yes, but once there, I'd have to park. I might even have to back up." She wasn't ready for backing up. Not on her first day.

"You can do it," he said and closed the door.

She glared at him for a full minute, but he didn't budge. That forced her to get behind the wheel and consider her options.

"I could just walk home," she said.

"What about your groceries?"

"You could carry some."

"But I won't."

He might not have screamed during their lessons, but he was very stubborn.

"Fine. I'll drive back, but if anything bad happens, you have to take over. And I'm seriously reconsidering the dinner I promised as a thank you."

"You don't have to do that. I was happy to help."

She looked at him. His eyes were dark and she couldn't tell what he was thinking. Maybe he didn't want to have dinner with her. After the way she'd overreacted to his kiss, who could blame him.

"I'd like to cook you dinner," she said. "But I'll understand if you don't want to come over."

"We're friends, right?"

She nodded.

"Then sure. I'll be there."

Friends. The way he said the word made her wonder if the statement had been to help him remember their relationship, or if it had been about telling her. Maybe he was making it clear that where she was concerned, he'd made his last move.

Jack arrived at Samantha's apartment exactly at seven. He'd brought Charlie, even though the dog was tired from his day and would only sleep. Still, if conversation got slow, they could always talk about the dog.

Pathetic, he told himself. He was completely pathetic. Yeah, he wanted to do the right thing where Samantha was concerned. Be a friend, a boss and let the rest of it go. But no matter what he told himself or how many times she rejected him, he couldn't seem to stop wanting her. Even now, standing outside of her door, he felt his body tighten in anticipation.

He knocked and promised himself that when he got home, he was going to figure out a way to get over her for good. But until then, a man could dream.

"You're here," she said as she opened the door and smiled at him.

"Was there any doubt?" he asked.

"I hoped there wasn't. Come on in."

He let Charlie lead the way, using the micro-second before he entered to brace himself to withstand the assault of color, gauzy fabric and perfume.

She'd changed out of her jeans and sweat-shirt—both covered in sewn-on flowers—and into a loose top and flowing skirt that nearly touched the top of her bare feet. She was a kaleidoscope of color, causing him not to know where to look first.

There was her hair, long and flowing and curly, but pinned up on one side. Her blouse that fell off one shoulder, exposing pale, creamy skin. Her feet with painted toes and at least two toe rings. Her arms, bare except for jingling bracelets.

"So you're back," he said.

She closed the door behind him. "What do you mean?"

"You've been a little conservative since you moved here. Oh sure, you've been playing basketball in the halls and wearing bright colors, but not in the way I remember. This is the first time you're exactly like you were."

She smiled. "That's about the nicest thing you've ever said to me. Thank you."

"You're welcome."

"Come on," she said, grabbing him by the arm and tugging him toward the kitchen. "I have wine and I'm going to let you be all macho and open it."

"It's what I live for."

They settled in the dining room with a bottle of wine and some appetizers. Charlie retreated to an ottoman where he curled up on the cushy surface and quickly went to sleep.

"I can get him down if you want," Jack said, jerking his head toward the dog. "He's great, but he sheds."

"No problem. A few dog hairs will make the condo seem more lived in. Right now it's still too perfect."

"And we wouldn't want that."

She dipped a chicken wing into spicy sauce. "Life's beauty is found in the irregular and unexpected. Ever see a perfect waterfall? A symmetrical sunset?"

"Technically the sun goes down in the same way every—" He broke off and grinned when she swatted him with the back of her hand.

"You know what I mean," she said. "I'm talking about the clouds, the colors and you know it."

"Maybe."

"My point is, dog hair is fine."

"Great. Maybe you'd like to take over grooming him, too."

"I wouldn't mind it. He's a great dog."

"I agree."

She sipped her wine. "I've noticed a bit more positive press in the past couple of days," she said. "There were at least two mentions of the upcoming advertisers' party. How Hanson Media Group is getting some things right."

SUSAN MALLERY   191

"I saw them, too. David is doing a hell of a job trying to counteract the negative stories."

"You really like him."

"In some ways he's more like my father than George ever was. Or maybe a big brother. He's not that much older than me. He was always there, making time in ways my father wouldn't. Even though he traveled a lot, he kept in touch. He took the time. Sometimes that's all that's required."

"I know." She grabbed for a piece of celery. "After my father walked out, I missed him terribly. Sure there was the whole trauma of going from the rich princess to the kid in castoffs, but it was more than that. Given the choice between getting the money back and getting my father back, I would have gladly picked him. But either he didn't get that or he didn't care."

"I know he walked out on your mom, but didn't he see you at all?"

She shook her head. "One day he was just gone. That played with my head. How was I supposed to believe my father had ever loved me when he walked away and never looked back?"

She sipped her wine. "Mom was great. She really fought him. Some of it was about the child support. It's crazy that a guy that wealthy paid almost nothing. But he could afford excellent lawyers and they knew all the tricks. As for seeing me, he would make promises and then not show up. There was always a good reason. Eventually my mom stopped pushing. She saw that it was hurting me more to hope."

Jack couldn't imagine what kind of man simply walked away from a child. His own father—no poster child for perfect parenting—had at least gone through the motions. He'd shown up to graduations and big events.

"It was his loss," he said.

"Thanks. I used to tell myself that, too. Most of the time I even believed it. I grew up determined not to repeat my mother's mistakes. I didn't care if the guy had money, as long as I was important to him and we wanted the same things."

Her words hit him hard. Ten years ago, he'd been that guy, but she hadn't been willing to see that, or maybe she'd just never thought of him as more than a friend.

"Vance?" he asked.

"I thought so. He'd been married before, so he was cautious. I liked that wariness. It made sense to me. I could tell he liked me a lot, but he wanted to take things slowly and I respected that, too. In hindsight, I was an idiot."

"In hindsight, we all are."

"Maybe. But I was a bigger idiot. He talked about how his first wife had been obsessed with how much money he made. She wanted the best, the biggest, the newest. I decided not to be like her, so I didn't ask for anything. It took me a while to figure out that had been his plan all along."

Jack didn't like the sound of that. "He set you up?"

"I think so." She sighed. "Yes, he did. It's hard for me to say that because it makes my choice even more crazy. He's a cardiologist in a big, successful practice. When we talked about getting married, he was concerned about losing that. I wanted to reassure him."

Jack grimaced. "Prenuptial?"

"Oh, yeah. I was sensible. I read the whole thing. But I didn't bother to get a lawyer. Why spend the money? Later, I realized he'd played me. He'd made a joke that his first wife was so stupid that she wouldn't have been able to get past the first page. But that I was really smart and would understand it all."

She shook her head. "I don't know if it was ego or my need to prove I wasn't her. Either way, I did read it, but I didn't get a lawyer to and I missed all the subtleties."

Jack practiced criminal law, but he'd heard

enough horror stories from co-workers practicing family law that he could guess the outcome.

"It wasn't what you thought."

"Not even close. Not only couldn't I touch his
practice or any income from it, but everything
of mine was community property. I got nothing
of his and he got half of mine. The only bright
spot is I didn't have a whole lot to take half of."

He reached across the table and covered her
hand with his. "I'm sorry."

"Don't be. I learned an important lesson. My
mother used to tell me the trick was to marry a
rich man and keep him. I think the real trick is
to not need a man at all."

"Speaking on behalf of my gender, we're not
all jerks."

"I know." She squeezed his fingers. "I blame
myself as much as Vance. There were warning
signs. I didn't pay much attention to them."

While he knew intellectually that she was
right—that she did have to take some respon-

sibility—his gut reaction was to hunt down Vance and beat the crap out of him. Talk about a low-life bastard.

"Want me to have someone look over the settlement and see if anything was missed?" he asked, suspecting she wouldn't appreciate the offer of physical violence.

"Thanks, but I'm okay. I'm doing my best to put my past behind me. It's been hard. Not because I'm so crazy about Vance, but because I tried to be so careful and he made a fool out of me in so many ways."

"Which makes you naturally wary," he said.

"Oh, yeah. Between him and my father, I'm now convinced any man I meet is out to screw me, and not in a sexual way." She grabbed another chicken wing.

"Ah, isn't this where you say present company excluded?" he asked.

She looked at him. "I want to. You're a great guy, Jack. I know that."

"But?"

"You're still a rich, powerful man. I'm having a little trouble letting go of that fact."

"I see your point. Here we sit, you thinking if you trust a guy he'll take off and dump on you in the process. I'm convinced anyone I care about will leave. We're not exactly a normal couple."

She grinned. "I like to think there is no normal."

"Do you believe that?"

"Sometimes. I know that I can't be afraid forever. I'm trying to get myself back." She tugged on the front of her blouse. "Dressing like this, for example. Vance hated my bohemian ways. He kept telling me I had to grow up."

Jack frowned. "Your free spirit is one of your best qualities. I'm sorry he didn't see that."

"Me, too. But there it is. He liked me to dress a certain way, that sort of thing."

"Controlling?"

She shrugged. "He was a cardiologist. He had an image."

"I know lawyers like that. It gets bad for their wives after they make partner. Suddenly what was great before isn't good enough anymore. I don't get it."

"That's because you're reasonable. Not everyone is." She released his hand and leaned back in her chair. "Now that you know the basic story of my pathetic divorce, I hope you'll understand why I'm becoming the queen of mixed messages where you're concerned. I know my past doesn't excuse my actions. I don't expect it to. I just hope you'll understand and accept my apology."

He stared at her. Until that second he'd never considered there was a reason for her behavior that had nothing to do with him.

"What?" she asked. "You have the strangest look on your face."

He shook his head. "I was just thinking that you being cautious around me was about you, not me. On the heels of that I realized I can't separate myself from who I am. I come from a wealthy family, I have a challenging, professional career. I am, on the surface, a walking, breathing manifestation of everything you're not looking for."

"Exactly."

At least she was being honest, he thought grimly. "A lot for us to overcome," he said, going for a light tone of voice. "I guess I should stop trying so hard."

She winced. "I feel really horrible. You've been nothing but nice to me. And before, in grad school, I loved us being close. You were terrific. I know in my head that you'd never hurt me."

"It's the rest of you that can't be convinced," he said.

"Yeah. But I've also decided it would be a good thing for me to face my fears."

While he liked the sound of that, he wasn't sure why she should bother. "You don't have to."

"It's the mature thing to do and I like to think of myself as mature. I want us to be friends."

Great. So much for making progress. "We *are* friends."

"I'm glad. I really love my job and I don't want to blow this opportunity."

"You won't," he told her.

"I hope not. It's just that…" She pressed her lips together and looked at him.

In any other woman, he would swear he was being given an invitation. But with Samantha? He wasn't sure. Better to stay on the safe side of the road.

"Remember that time we were studying in the park and that woman's dog got away from her?" he asked. "She was running around calling for him and you said we had to help."

She grinned. "Yes. And you told me that a dog would never come to strangers so I said we had to tempt it with food. So we went to that butcher and bought bones."

He'd felt like an idiot, he thought, but he'd been with Samantha so he hadn't cared.

"There we were, running around, calling for a dog and throwing bones around. Every stray in a three-mile radius started following us."

"It was sad," she said. "I felt so badly for those dogs."

"You felt badly? You're the one who insisted we find a rescue place for them. Then it was my car we crammed them into. Of course you hadn't realized that dogs like to mark what they think of as new territory."

She winced. "I felt really horrible about the smell, but the dogs got adopted. So that's something."

"Unfortunately none of the new owners was willing to buy my smelly car."

He'd been forced to get rid of it for practically nothing. Still, it had been worth it, he thought, remembering how happy she'd been about the dogs.

She leaned close. "Doesn't taking the moral high ground ease some of the financial sting?"

"Not as much as you'd think," he said, finding his gaze riveted on her mouth.

Dumb idea, he told himself. On a scale of one to ten, ten being somewhere between stupid and idiotic, this was a twelve.

But there was something about the way she smiled and the light in her eyes. Something that spoke of promise and desire.

Hadn't he always been an idiot where she was concerned?

He shifted toward her and lightly touched her cheek with his fingers. He thought that if he gave her plenty of warning, she would have time to bolt before he kissed her.

But she didn't. Instead she parted her lips slightly and drew in a quick breath.

He took that as a yes and kissed her.

He moved slowly, only touching her mouth with the lightest of brushes. He kept his hands to himself, or at least didn't do more than rest one on her shoulder and the other on her arm. He waited for her to kiss back.

And waited. One heartbeat. Two. Then slowly, almost tentatively, her lips moved on his. She pressed a little harder, then touched his bottom lip with the very tip of her tongue.

It was as if she'd just taken a blowtorch to his bloodstream. Heat and need exploded and he was instantly hard. He'd heard that it took longer for a man to get aroused as he got older. Apparently he hadn't crossed that threshold yet.

But as much as he wanted to pull her close, to rub his hands all over her until she was wet and weak and begging him to take her, as much as he wanted to take off her clothes and run his tongue over every inch of her, he did nothing. He sat there letting her take control of their kiss. Let her set the pace.

When she touched the tip of her tongue to his

lip again, he tilted his head and parted for her. She slipped into his mouth and traced the inside of his lower lip.

Everything got hotter, harder and more intense. The need to take control, to claim her, threatened to overwhelm him, but he was determined not to screw up again. She'd made it clear that he pushed all her buttons, so it made sense to go slowly.

But when she circled his tongue with hers and sighed, it took every bit of self-control he had not to reach for her. Instead he mentally ground his teeth in frustration. He kissed her back, but slowly, without letting her know how deep the passion flowed. And when she withdrew slightly, he straightened, as if he were unaffected by what they'd just done.

She ducked her head and smiled. "That was nice."

"Yes, it was."

She glanced at him from under her lashes.

"I'm a complete adult and I accept responsibility for what just happened."

Was that her way of saying she wasn't going to back off and run this time?

"And?" he asked, knowing there had to be a punch line.

"No *and*. Just that. And me saying thanks for being patient."

"My pleasure." Although pleasure didn't exactly describe his painful state of arousal. He reached for another chicken wing and bit into it. In time, the need would fade to a manageable level. His erection would cease to throb with each beat of his heart and the temperature in his body would slowly cool. But until then, life was hell.

"You're going to have to go to a few Cubs games when the season starts," he said.

She laughed. "You're deliberately changing the subject."

"You noticed."

She smiled. "This is in an effort to erase the tension here and keep me from feeling awkward."

"Something like that." Some of his motivation was selfish. Thinking about baseball was a time-honored way to keep from thinking about sex.

Her smiled widened. "Okay. Then tell me everything you know about the Cubs."

"At least the news isn't getting worse," David said.

"Not exactly the sign of forward progress I would like," Jack said. "But it beats the hell out of our string of bad news. You've been working hard to get us favorable play in the press."

"It's my job."

Jack leaned back on the sofa in his uncle's office. "Helen came to see me last week. She wanted to talk about how I was doing. It was almost as if…"

David raised his eyebrows but didn't speak.

Jack shook his head. "It was almost as if she was worried about me."

"Is that impossible to believe?"

"Yes. Why would she care?"

"Why wouldn't she? You don't know anything about Helen."

"Do you?"

"Not really. George and I haven't been exactly tight these past few years. But I've spoken with her, spent a few dinners with her. She seems reasonable and intelligent. You might want to take the time to get to know her."

"That's what Samantha says. She's a serious advocate."

David smiled.

Jack narrowed his gaze. "What?"

His uncle's smile turned into a grin. "There's something about the way you say her name. So things are progressing."

"No and no. We're getting along. She works for me. That's it."

"Like I believe that."

"It's true. She is just getting over a divorce. I'm not interested in getting involved in that process."

"Have you considered the fact that you already are?"

Was he? Jack thought about the weekend, when he and Samantha had spent so much time together. Hearing about her past and her marriage made a lot of things more clear to him. But that didn't mean he was interested in her. Not in any way but sexually.

"I'm not involved," he told David.

His uncle nodded. "Keep telling yourself that. Eventually it will be true."

Chapter Eight

The company had gone all out for the advertisers' party. As this was the first one Samantha had attended, she didn't know if the stunning decorations, incredible view and fabulous food were normal or if this party was a little bit extra-special in an effort to soothe their accounts.

Either way, she was excited to be there and felt just like Cinderella at the ball. For once, she'd left her loose and comfy clothes behind and had instead worn a formfitting strapless gown in dark apple-green.

The shimmering fabric very nearly matched the color of her eyes. She'd gone simple in the jewelry department, wearing vintage paste earrings that looked like amazing diamonds. The antique settings made them look like the genuine article. Last, she'd spent nearly two hours on her hair, curling it on big rollers and then drying it. But the effort had been worth it. Her normally tight, natural curls were now loose and sexy. She'd pinned up the sides and left the back to cascade over her shoulder blades.

She felt good and knew she looked her best. The question was had she done enough to dazzle Jack?

"Not that I care," she murmured as she made her way to the bar for the glass of white wine she would hold on to for most of the evening. She refused to define herself by a man.

Not that she was. Wanting to knock Jack's socks off had nothing to do with definition and everything to do with the fire she'd seen in his eyes last weekend when they'd kissed.

She saw David and moved toward him. It was early and most of the guests hadn't arrived.

"You look beautiful," he said with a smile.

"Thank you. Great place. I love the view."

From one set of floor-to-ceiling windows was the lake and from the other were the lights of the city.

"We have a lot on the line," David told her. "Are you rethinking your decision to take this job? This isn't Hanson Media Group's most shining moment."

"Jack asked me that as well. I meant what I said then. I'm excited about the opportunity to create something wonderful."

"I've seen the preliminary designs on the Web site. They're great. And I've been over the security you want to put in place. It could be called obsessive."

She laughed. "I'm sure I'll hear worse before

the launch. The point is to make this a safe destination for children. I'm willing to do everything possible to make that happen. Even if it means driving the IT guys a little crazy."

David grinned. "Good for you. Next week let's set up a meeting to talk about publicity for the launch. I've already reserved some space in a couple of kid magazines and there will be a few Saturday morning cartoon spots."

Samantha stared at him. "Television advertising?" She knew how much it cost.

"Jack said you were going to be the one to save the company. So he told me to think big."

She doubted Jack had ever said she would save the company but she knew the Web site could go a long way to boosting the bottom line. Still, she was surprised and pleased to find out how much he was supporting her.

"I'll call you," she said. "I have a lot of ideas for the advertising."

"Why am I not surprised?"

She laughed. "I have ideas for pretty much everything."

"That's what Jack said."

There was something in David's voice that made her wonder what else Jack had been saying about her. Not that she would ask.

Several clients walked into the ballroom. David excused himself and went over to greet them. Samantha followed more slowly, wanting to give him a moment to talk before she moved close and introduced herself.

She'd done plenty of industry parties. They had a simple formula for success. She had to make sure she spoke with everyone, was charming and friendly and remembered their names. Then, during the second half of the evening, she needed to circulate, chatting about anything and finding subtle ways to talk up the company. She'd also learned to pay attention to anyone who seemed to be on his or her own. Being lonely at a party was never a good idea.

Taking a little time to be a friend and then introduce the shy person to others went a long way to making the evening a success.

David spoke with the group of eight men and women. She waited for a lull in the conversation then moved in closer.

David smiled at her. "This is Samantha Edwards, one of our newest and brightest additions to Hanson Media Group. Samantha is working on an incredible expansion of our Internet site for kids."

One of the women raised her eyebrows. "Do I want my children spending more time on the computer?"

Samantha smiled. "Probably not. Aren't they on there so much now?"

The woman nodded.

"It's a real problem," Samantha told her. "One I've been working on. My goal isn't to trap them inside for more hours, but to make their computer time more efficient, fun and safe, all the while making sure their homework gets done and their parents are happy."

"That's a big order," one of the men said. "Can you do it?"

She nodded. "Absolutely. Let me tell you how in two minutes or less."

She launched into the pitch she'd spent the last week perfecting, then stayed long enough to answer a few questions. When the group had moved away to sample the buffet, David took her by the elbow.

"Well done," he said.

"I believe in being prepared."

"Good. Let's go over here. I have some more people I want you to meet."

About an hour later, Samantha felt a distinct tingling on the back of her neck. Careful to continue to pay attention to the conversation, she casually looked around to find the source of her hyperawareness.

It didn't take her long to locate Jack standing by the window with two older men.

At the sight of him, she felt her blood surge a little faster. Her skin seemed to heat as her toes curled.

He looked pretty amazing in his tailored tux, but then he had the James Bond sort of good looks that were made for formal wear. The stark white of his shirt contrasted with his black tie.

Yummy, she thought, instantly recalling the kiss they'd shared and how her body had reacted to his nearness. Despite the fears left over from her previous marriage and her general wariness of men like Jack, she found herself wanting a repeat of their make-out session along with the time and privacy to take things further.

She forced her attention back on the conversation and away from Jack. After a few minutes, the tingle increased, then she felt a warm hand on the small of her back.

"Having a good time?" he asked everyone, even as he continued to touch her.

"Great party," Melinda Myers, the president of the largest string of car dealerships in the Midwest said. "Your father would be very proud, Jack."

Samantha guessed she was the only one who felt him stiffen slightly.

"Thank you," he said graciously. "Despite everything that has happened recently, I wanted to keep the family tradition going. Your business has been very important to us."

Melinda smiled. "Hanson Media Group has been a good partner for me. I don't want that to change."

"Nor do I," he told her.

Melinda nodded at Samantha. "I've been hearing great things about the new Internet site. Impressive. Samantha was just telling me about her plans and some innovative ways for my company to be a part of it."

"I hope you take her up on her offer," Jack said.

Melinda smiled coyly. "Of course I will. I know a good deal when I hear one. That's how I got to where I am now."

Samantha did her best to pay attention to the banter but it was difficult with Jack's fingers pressing against her skin. Heat radiated out from him, feeling hot enough to burn.

Warmth spread out in all directions, making her breasts swell and her thighs melt. She wanted to blame her reaction on the liquor, but she'd yet to take more than a sip of her wine. Her next best excuse was that she hadn't had much to eat that day.

A tall older man approached and asked Melinda to dance. Several other people excused themselves, leaving Samantha and Jack standing together beside the dance floor.

"So what do you think?" he asked, his dark eyes locking with hers.

She assumed he meant about the party and

not her awareness of him. "The night is a hit," she said. "I had wondered how our advertisers would react to all the recent bad news, but they're taking it in stride. A lot of that is you." She grimaced. "I'm sorry. I know you don't want to hear that, but it's true. They see you as a capable replacement for your father."

"Nice to know they think I can do as well as a man who defrauded investors."

She touched his arm. "They don't mean it that way."

"I know." He set down his glass on a nearby tray. "Want to dance?"

She would never have thought he was the type to be comfortable on the dance floor and, to be honest, the thought of being that close to him was two parts thrilling and one part pure torture. Still, she'd never been able to resist things that were bad for her.

She set down her wine. "Absolutely."

He took her hand and led her to the edge of

the parquet dance floor, then drew her into his arms. She went easily, finding the sense of being against him and swaying to music almost familiar. Had they done this before? In grad school? She didn't remember a specific time when they'd—

"You're frowning," he said. "I'll admit my moves are pretty basic, but I didn't think they were frown-inducing."

"What? Oh. Sorry. I was trying to remember if we'd ever danced together before."

"We haven't."

"You sound so sure of yourself."

"I am. I would have remembered."

Which meant what? But rather than pursue the question, she drew in a deep breath and consciously relaxed into the rhythm of the music.

The slow song allowed them to sway together, touching from shoulder to thigh. He clasped one of her hands while her other rested on his shoulder.

"Did I mention you look stunning?" he asked, his voice a low murmur in her ear.

"No, and because of that, I think you should have to say it at least twice."

"You look stunning. The dress is nearly as beautiful as the woman wearing it."

Ooh, talk about smooth. He certainly was a man who knew his way around a compliment. "I don't get much chance to dress up these days. It's fun for a change."

"And worth the wait."

The song ended, leaving her feeling as if she wanted more. A lot more. But this was a work-related party and she still had rounds to make, as did Jack.

"I'm off to dazzle," she said. "Thanks for the dance."

"You're welcome."

He held her gaze a second longer than nec-essary, and in that heartbeat of time, she felt her body flush with need. All the tingles and whispers and little touches combined into an unexpected wave of sexual desire.

Then Jack turned and disappeared into the crowd.

She stared after him, trying to remember the last time she'd felt safe enough to want a man. She'd spent the last two years of her marriage simply going through the motions of intimacy because it had been expected, but she hadn't enjoyed herself. She'd been too hurt and broken to let herself feel anything.

Had time begun to heal her wounds or was her reaction specifically about Jack? She knew what it was like to make love with him. The memory of their single night together had been burned into her brain. She remembered everything from the way he'd kissed her to the feel of him inside of her. He'd coaxed more orgasms from her that night than she'd had in the previous year.

Funny how a month ago she would have

sworn she would never be interested in getting physical with a guy again in her life. But suddenly there were possibilities. Maybe not with anyone else, but certainly with Jack.

Jack didn't bother counting the number of times he was compared with his father and told he was nearly as great as the old man had been. He couldn't believe so many people could know about his father's mismanaging of the company and still call him a good man.

By eleven, he was tired and ready to be done with the party. But there were more advertisers to schmooze and more hands to shake. It came with the job.

Helen walked over and offered him a glass of scotch. "How are you holding up?" she asked.

She looked beautiful in a fitted gown that showed off perfect curves. Her blond hair had been piled on her head, giving her a regal air. He didn't doubt there were plenty of men willing to take her home for the night, or as long as they could get.

Had she done that? She was substantially younger than his father. Had she taken lovers to keep herself satisfied?

Then he pushed the thought away. Why was he once again assuming the worst about her? He'd lived in the city and traveled in similar social circles as his father and Helen. There'd never been a whisper of gossip about either of them.

"Not my idea of a good time," he said. "What about you?"

She glanced around the crowd and shrugged. "Last year I came with George. I can't stop thinking about that and I keep expecting to turn around and see him. It's difficult."

She took a sip of her drink. As she shifted and the light spilled across her face, he could've sworn he saw tears in her eyes.

He did swear, silently, calling himself several

choice names for his earlier thoughts. "You really loved him."

"Stop sounding so surprised when you say that," she told him. "Of course I loved him. I'm very intelligent and very capable. I didn't need to marry someone to get what I wanted from life. I could have done that on my own."

He wanted to ask why his father. What qualities had the old man shown her that he'd managed to keep from his sons?

"They're saying good things about you," she said. "They're happy you're in charge."

"So that sharp clanging sound I hear is the door closing on my freedom?"

"I don't know," she told him. "No one wants you to keep a job you hate."

"Except the board of directors."

"It's not their job to be compassionate. I suspect, over time, they would come to see that an unhappy president wouldn't be best for Hanson Media Group."

"I don't think I have that much time."

"You could be right." She took another sip from her drink. "I saw you dancing with Samantha. You make a very attractive couple."

"She's a beautiful woman."

"And a friend. You're a great guy, Jack, but I know how you are. Serial monogamy is great in theory, but sometimes someone gets hurt."

She wasn't being subtle. "You don't want that person to be Samantha."

"She's just been through a difficult time."

"I know about her divorce."

Helen smiled. "I wonder if you really do."

"What do you mean?"

"Be kind to my friend."

"I'll do my best." He shook his head. "You put her name on the short list. I'd wondered how it got there."

"I knew she would do a good job and I thought she was someone you could trust."

There was something in her voice that

implied she knew more than she was saying. How much had Samantha told her about their previous relationship?

"Good call on your part," he said.

"Thanks. I have my moments." She looked around at the large gathering. "Ready to plunge back into the hordes?"

"No, but there's not much choice."

She glanced back at him. "I know you don't care or even want to hear this, but your father would have been very proud of you."

He didn't say anything because he was starting to like and respect Helen, but as she walked away he acknowledged she was right. He didn't care about what his father thought.

Samantha knew she was babbling. It was late, she was tired and hungry and she couldn't seem to stop talking.

"I think the party had a real positive impact on our relationships with our advertisers," she said as Jack stopped at a light. "There was so much good feedback and I have some great ideas to bring to the next creative meeting for the Web site."

He drove through the quiet, empty streets, nodding every now and then. She knew neither of them was really interested in business and that he already knew everything she was saying.

"The band was good, too," she added with a bright smile. "A lot of people were dancing. That doesn't usually happen at parties like this. But everyone seemed really relaxed. Didn't you think so? Weren't you relaxed?"

He stopped for another light and turned to glance at her. "You don't have to entertain me on the drive home," he said. "It's okay if we don't talk."

Great. So she'd bored him.

She firmly pressed her lips together and vowed not to say another word between here and the parking garage at their building. From there it was a short elevator ride to her condo.

Silence, she told herself. She could do silence.

"I like your car," she said before she could stop herself. "Is it new?"

"About two years old. Why are you so nervous?"

"Me? I'm not. I'm fine. I had a good time tonight."

"You sure didn't drink. As far as I could tell you didn't eat. So what's going on?"

"Nothing. I'm fine. Perfectly. See? This is me being fine."

He pulled into the parking garage and drove to his space. When he turned off the engine, he shifted so that he faced her.

"Are you worried I'm going to make a pass at you?" he asked.

The blunt question shocked her into silence. If she looked at things from the right perspective, life sure had a sense of humor. For the past few weeks she'd been hoping Jack wouldn't notice her as anything but a co-worker. Now she wanted him to see her as a desirable woman and he was worried she thought he was going to come on to her. Which meant he wasn't.

She'd spent the entire evening in shoes that made her feet hurt for nothing.

"Why would I worry about that?" she asked, not able to meet his gaze.

"Because of what happened the last time we were alone together."

Ah, yes. That magical kiss. "It was nice," she whispered.

"I thought so, too. Still do." He leaned across her and opened her door. "Come on. I'll walk you home."

He came around and helped her out of the car, then took her hand as they walked to the elevator. Seconds later the doors opened and they stepped inside.

She wanted to say something. Maybe invite him inside or at least come off as cool and sophisticated. But she couldn't think of anything good and she didn't know how to tell him she wasn't exactly ready for the evening to be over. Maybe in her next life she would understand men and deal with them better. In this one, she was batting a big, fat zero.

The elevator stopped on her floor. She turned to say good-night, only he was stepping off the elevator and leading her to her door.

She dug for her key in her tiny evening bag and clutched it in her hand.

Her place was at the end of the hall. Jack took the key from her, opened the door then cupped her face and smiled at her.

"You've told me no plenty of times," he said quietly. "Tonight your eyes are saying something different. Which should I believe? Your words or your eyes?"

Her stomach flipped over, her throat went dry

and it was all she could do to keep hanging on to her purse.

It all came down to this. What did she want from Jack?

"Talk has always been overrated," she whispered.

"I agree," he said as he eased her into the condo and closed the door behind them.

She heard the lock turn just before he bent down and kissed her.

She instinctively leaned into him, wanting to feel his mouth on hers. When his lips brushed against her mouth, she wrapped her arms around his neck to hold him in place.

They surged together, need growing until her mind overflowed with images of them together, naked, craving. Even as she tilted her head and parted her lips, she dropped her purse on the floor and stepped out of her shoes.

He took advantage of her invitation with a quickness that heated her blood. He nipped at her lower lip, then swept his tongue into her mouth where he claimed her with an eagerness that made her thighs tremble.

His hands were everywhere. Her shoulders, her bare arms, her back. She touched him, as well, stroking the breadth of his shoulders, before starting to tug on his jacket.

He quickly shrugged out of it, letting it fall, then he pulled off his tie. He broke the kiss, then turned her so her back was to him.

"Cuffs," he murmured as he pushed her hair over her right shoulder, then held out his hands in front of her.

But removing the gold-and-diamond cuff links was more difficult than it should have been. Even as she reached for the fastening, he nibbled on her bare shoulder, then licked the same spot.

Goose bumps erupted on her arms. Her nipples got hard and she felt the first telltale wetness on her panties.

At last she managed to free the cuff links.

She started to turn, but he stayed behind her, put his hands on her hips and drew her back against him.

He was already hard. She felt the thickness of his need as he rubbed back and forth. Wanting filled her, turning her body liquid. He moved his hands up her body until he cupped her breasts.

Her curves were modest at best, but exquisitely sensitive. Even through the fabric, she felt his thumbs brush over her nipples in a way designed to make her his slave.

"I've wanted to do this all evening," he breathed before biting down on her earlobe. "That damn dress. You were driving me crazy. I couldn't decide which would be more erotic—coming up behind you and touching you like this or just saying, 'The hell with it,' and shoving my hand down the front of your dress."

Either would have taken her breath away.

"I want you naked," he murmured as he kissed her neck. "I want to touch you all over until we're both exhausted and then I want to do it all again."

He'd talked to her before, she remembered, her brain turning mushy from too many hormones and too little sex. She hadn't been with a lot of men, but except for Jack, they'd all been silent.

She loved his words. They not only turned her on, but they left no doubt that she did the same to him.

She turned in his arms and pressed her mouth to his. He kissed her with an intensity that shook her to the core. When she felt his fingers on her zipper, she trembled in anticipation of being naked with him.

Her dress fell in a whisper of silk. Underneath she wore tiny panties and nothing else. He continued to kiss her even as he brought his hands around to cup her breasts.

While she'd always wanted to be voluptuous, she had a theory that her small breasts had the same number of nerve endings as big ones, so hers were more sensitive. Apparently Jack remembered, because he touched her gently as he stroked her hot skin.

Fiery sensation shot through her, making it hard to keep breathing. Every part of her being focused on his touch as he moved closer and closer to her nipples. At last he touched them, first with just his fingertips. He lightly rubbed the very tips before squeezing them oh so gently.

She gasped with pleasure. He groaned, then broke the kiss and pushed her back. Seconds later three books, her mail and a plastic container of fake flowers crashed to the floor. Before she could figure out what he was doing, he lifted her onto the top of the wood console in her foyer, bent his head and sucked on one of her nipples.

Suddenly the mess didn't matter at all. She closed her eyes and arched her chest toward him. Her fingers tangled in his hair.

"More," she breathed as he circled her tight, quivery flesh. "Don't stop."

He didn't. He sucked and licked and circled and then moved to her other breast. He replaced tongue with fingers, arousing her with everything he did.

He put one of his hands on her thigh and moved it steadily toward her center. She parted her legs, then cursed the panties still in place as he rubbed her through the silk.

"Off," she begged, shifting on the console. "I need them off."

He grabbed them and pulled them down. When she was fully naked, he reached for her and slid his fingers into her swollen, waiting heat.

Heaven, she thought, barely able to breathe. Heaven and then some. He explored her, quickly finding her favorite spot, then teasing it. He shifted so that his thumb rubbed there and his first two fingers could slip inside of her.

Passion grew as her body tensed. She clung

to him, barely able to absorb all the sensations. It was too fast, too soon. And yet…

"Jack," she breathed as she felt herself spinning higher and higher.

His only response was to suck harder on her breasts. The combination of pleasures was too much, she thought as she felt the first shuddering release of her climax. It overtook her body, leaving her unable to do anything but hold on for the ride.

She felt herself tighten around his fingers. He moved in and out, imitating the act of love. Toward the end, he raised his head and kissed her on the mouth. She kissed him back, then sighed as her contractions slowed.

She opened her eyes and smiled at him. "Wow," she breathed, both pleased and a little embarrassed at the speed of her response.

He grinned and then picked her up in his arms. She shrieked and wrapped her arms around his neck.

"What are you doing?" she asked.

"Taking a naked woman to bed. What does it look like?"

"A plan I can get into," she said, then lightly bit his earlobe. "Once we're there, you can get into me."

"I will," he promised. "In a second."

"What do you… Oh!"

He dropped her onto the bed, then quickly stripped out of his clothes. She gave herself over to the show, remembering how good he'd looked before.

Time had been kind. He still had a hard, sculpted body and his arousal was very impressive. She reached for him as he joined her on the bed, but he shook his head.

"Protection?" he asked.

She pointed at the nightstand and held back the need to explain that they were, in fact, very new. She'd bought them the day after he'd kissed her. More than a little wishful thinking on her part.

He pulled out the box of condoms and removed one. But instead of putting it on, he slipped between her legs and knelt over her.

"I want you," he said.

She saw the desire in his eyes and felt her body quicken with an answering need.

"Me, too. Despite my recent thrill ride."

"Good."

He bent down and kissed her belly. As he moved south, she knew what he was going to do. Politeness dictated that she at least offer him his own release before taking another of her own, but as she tried to speak, she remembered what it had been like that one night they'd spent together. How he'd kissed her so intimately, with an understanding of her body that had taken her to paradise so quickly.

"Just for a couple of minutes," she told him as he pressed his mouth against her. "Three at most."

He chuckled. She felt the movement and the puff of warm air. Then his tongue swept against her with the exact amount of pressure. He circled her most sensitive spot once, twice, before brushing it with the flat part of his tongue.

She was lost. Rude or not, she couldn't stand the thought of stopping him. Not when he made her feel so good. She pulled her knees up and spread her legs apart, then she dug her heels into the bed.

He moved faster, pressing a tiny bit harder. It was the most intimate act she knew and she'd trusted no one but him to do this to her. She might have trusted Vance, but he'd claimed it was disgusting, although he'd been plenty willing for her to do it to him.

Without warning, her body shuddered into orgasm. She lost control in a way she never had before. He kissed and licked and moved his fingers back and forth as she screamed her release into the night.

She lost track of time and reality. There was only the waves and waves of pleasure filling her. At last her body slowed. She felt him pull back. She reached toward him, not wanting to lose the connection, but then he was there, between her legs, pushing, filling her.

She opened her eyes as he slowly thrust himself inside of her. He was much bigger than his fingers and she felt herself stretching. The delicious pressure made her shudder again and again. She came with each thrust, milking him.

He braced himself on the bed and made love to her. Their eyes locked and she watched him get closer and closer. She wrapped her legs around his hips, holding him inside, feeling him climax and contracting around him as he did.

Chapter Nine

Jack opened the drapes and returned to the bed to watch the growing light creep across the room. He gently shifted the lock of hair curling across Samantha's cheek so that he could see the pale skin and the curve of her mouth.

She was beautiful, which wasn't news, but still struck him this morning. She lay across rumpled sheets, with the blanket tangled in her legs. Her bare arm stretched toward him and he could see her naked right breast.

Just looking at the tight nipple sent blood

surging to his groin. He wanted her again, but after last night, he didn't think he should indulge himself. Three times was impressive, four was greedy. Besides, he didn't want to make her sore.

He touched her curls again, rubbing his fingers against the soft texture of her hair. He didn't even have to close his eyes to remember what it had been like the second time, when she'd straddled him, claiming him, moving faster and faster as her body gave itself over to pleasure.

He'd watched her as she'd arched her back, her breasts thrusting toward him, her hair spilling down, swaying with each thrust of her hips.

They were good together, at least in bed. But would she see that? Or would she revert to type—second-guessing what had happened and telling them both that this was all a mistake?

She stirred slightly, then rolled onto her back

and opened her eyes. The sheet pooled around her waist, leaving her breasts bare and even after she'd seen him, she didn't try to cover herself.

"Good morning," she whispered. "Did you sleep?"

He nodded.

Her mouth curved into a smile. "You're looking so serious. What's wrong?"

"I'm fine."

She rolled toward him and touched his bare chest. "Then what?" she asked, her smile fading. "Are you sorry about last night?"

"That's your line."

"Oh."

He saw the hurt flash in her eyes and groaned. "Samantha, no. I didn't mean it like that."

She sat up and pulled the sheet so she was covered to her shoulders. Her messy hair tumbled across her bare shoulders and her mouth twisted.

"You did mean it like that and you have every

right to expect me to bolt," she said firmly. "Based on how I've been acting, what else could you think? I'm sorry I was a total change-o girl."

He stared at her. "A what?"

"You know what I mean. I've been the queen of sending mixed messages. I hated that I was doing it and I didn't know how to stop. I've since given myself a stern talking to. I'm working on being in the moment and letting the future take care of itself. You've been nothing but terrific since I moved to Chicago. You're a great guy and I have no regrets about last night." She shook her head. "I take that back. I have one regret. That it took me so long to get you into bed."

He'd braced himself to hear a lot of things, but that wasn't one of them. "You're not sorry."

"Nope. Are you?"

He grinned. "Are you kidding? Last night was incredible."

"I do have a special talent," she said modestly,

then smiled. "Okay, what happens now? What are your usual rules of play."

"You assume I have rules."

"All guys do. Tell me what they are and I'll tell you if I agree."

Dangerous territory, he thought. Although maybe not. Samantha was coming off a rough divorce. He doubted she was looking for anything serious any more than he was.

"Serial monogamy," he said. "We stay together as long as it's good. No forever, no hurt feelings when it's over."

She batted her eyes. "So you'd be, like, my boyfriend."

He chuckled. "If that's what you want to call it."

"Would we get matching tattoos?"

"Never."

"Would we make love?"

"Almost constantly."

She flopped back on the bed. "What makes you think I want you?"

"Last night you were screaming."

Her cheeks darkened with color. "I don't remember that."

"Trust me. You screamed."

Her humor faded. "You've been really patient with me, Jack. I've been so scared about messing up and being taken. I thought it was best to just avoid any kind of relationship. But that's no way to live. Complicating the situation was my reaction to you."

He took her hand in his and rubbed her fingers with his thumb. "What reaction?"

"You know, mine."

"You have to be a little more specific."

She sighed. "Look at the situation logically. If I didn't want to get involved, why didn't I just stay away from you? Why did I keep coming back for more?" She shrugged. "You've always been something of a temptation."

He liked the sound of that. "Since when?"

"Since before. When we were in grad school."

What? "You blew me off. You said it was a mistake."

"I was scared."

"Not of me. What did I ever do wrong?"

"Nothing. That's my point. My fears were about me. But even they weren't enough to keep me away. I was so torn. You were a lot like my father in that whole rich, powerful way and I didn't know how to handle it."

Which meant he was also like her ex-husband. How did he convince her that he wasn't the enemy? That he wasn't interested in hurting her?

"I never forgot that night we shared," she said, not quite meeting his gaze. "After a while I convinced myself that I'd made it better than it was in my mind. That no one was that good. After last night, I know I was wrong."

He wanted to tell her that their incredible time in bed together had a whole lot more to do with chemistry than with him, but it was kind of nice having her think he was special.

"At least half of last night was about you," he said. "You're very responsive."

"Not all the time. Pretty much only here. So is this okay? Is this what you want?"

He nodded. "I'll be your boyfriend."

She laughed. "That sounds nice. I could use a little normal in my life right now."

"Normal?" He moved in close and pressed his lips against her ear. "Not normal. I have some very kinky fantasies in mind."

"Really? Like what?"

Samantha finished her speech to nods and smiles. She collected her materials and returned to her seat at the side of the room.

This had been her first ever presentation to a board of directors and it had been pretty high up on the nightmare scale.

"Sort of like facing down seven stern principals in school?" David asked in a low voice.

"Worse," she whispered. "Do they all have to look so disapproving?"

"It comes with being on the board. They're supposed to take things very seriously."

"Obviously. I'm just glad I wasn't trying to do stand-up."

She reached for her cup of coffee and swallowed the tepid liquid. When this was all over, she owed Jack a big apology. He'd insisted everyone practice their presentations several times before the board meeting. They had all endured long evenings, perfecting their pitches.

At the time, she'd thought his anal obsession was foolish. Wouldn't spontaneity be more interesting? But having just endured the stern expressions and pointed questions, she realized the importance of being prepared.

"I'm up next," David said as he was called.

Samantha leaned back in her chair and did her best to relax. She'd heard all the talks so many times, she knew what to expect and could tune out the words. So she found herself with a little time on her hands.

She used it to good advantage, turning her head so she caught sight of Jack sitting at the end of the long conference table.

He looked good—all buttoned up and formal in his black suit. If she didn't know him, he could have seriously intimidated her. But she did know him—every inch of him. And there were some mighty fine inches.

She watched the way he listened intently—as if he hadn't heard every sentence at least a dozen times—and took notes.

He was a great guy, she thought happily. Smart, caring, funny. The man owned a dog. How was she supposed to resist that? If she hadn't known about—

Samantha stiffened in her seat as a single thought flashed through her brain, on and off, over and over again. She wasn't able to think about anything else, and as she considered the truth of the statement, she wondered what on earth she was supposed to do about it.

Jack wasn't just some guy she'd hooked up with. He wasn't just an old friend or a new boss or a terrific lover. He was all that and much more.

He was the one who got away.

The board meeting was endless and three kinds of torture, Jack thought when the presentations finally finished. The board excused everyone but Helen and him. He thanked his team as they left and braced himself for the inevitable confrontation. He'd put it off as long as he could, but there was no going back now.

Baynes, the chairman, waited until the door closed before looking at Jack. "You've pulled the team together. I'm impressed."

Jack nodded, but didn't speak.

"Obviously our goal is to keep Hanson Media Group alive. Between the bad stories in the press and troubles internally, that's a challenge. You're well on your way here. The new programs are very exciting. But we need to do more. We need to provide stability over the long haul."

Several of the board members nodded in agreement. Helen shook her head.

"We don't have to do anything right now," she said. "I know where you're going and it's too soon. If we simply announce Jack as the new president, it will be seen as a knee-jerk reaction. Let's think this through."

Samantha might sing her friend's praises, but obviously Helen, like the board, was ready to sell him out if that's what was best for Hanson Media Group.

"Helen, it's necessary. Do you want to see George's legacy bankrupt, or worse, lost in some mega-conglomerate takeover?" Baynes shrugged. "I don't. The only way to keep Hanson Media Group going is to announce a permanent president. Jack, I know you're anxious to get back to your law practice, but we all have to make sacrifices. It's time for you to make one. I'm asking you to accept the job."

Jack looked at the older man. "What sacrifices are being made aside from mine?" he asked calmly.

"You know what I mean," Baynes told him.

"Actually, I don't. I'm not interested in running Hanson Media Group any longer than the three months I've already agreed to."

Several of the board members started speaking at once.

"This is a family company. Always has been. You owe it to your father."

Not an argument designed to get his vote, Jack thought grimly.

"Think of the stockholders. What about them?"

"You're the best man for the job. The only man."

Baynes quieted them. "Jack, your family owns

the largest percentage of stock, but we still have an obligation to the financial community."

"I find it hard to believe you can't come up with a single qualified person to take over this company," Jack said. "Have you even been looking?"

"You're the one we want."

"Has it occurred to any of you that forcing Jack to stay when he doesn't want to is incredibly foolish?" Helen asked. "Someone unhappy in the position isn't to anyone's advantage. Now if he wanted to be here…"

"I don't," Jack said flatly.

Baynes narrowed his gaze. "I would think you, Helen, of all people would want a family member in charge of the company."

She leaned forward. "I agree that Jack is very qualified and I trust him implicitly. But I see no advantage in guilting him into staying on. It's a short-term solution and I don't want that. We're doing fine for the moment. Let's not make a change before we have to. Leave Jack alone to do his job. In the meantime, we can be looking for a suitable replacement. If there isn't one, then Jack gets my vote."

"I don't like it," Baynes said.

"Just so we're all clear," Helen continued, "until George's will is read, I control his voting stock, which means I get the final say." She looked at Jack. "I still believe you owe your father but I'm reluctant to put his legacy in the hands of someone who doesn't respect his vision."

Not respecting his father's vision was the least of it, Jack thought. But before he could protest, Baynes cut in.

"What do you know about the will?" he asked Helen.

"Nothing," she said. "I'll find out when everyone else does. That's not my point. We have time to think this through and make the right decision for Hanson Media Group. As

long as the company is moving in the right direction, then I say let it be."

Samantha paced the length of Jack's office,
then turned around and walked back the other
way. He'd already been in with the board for
nearly twenty minutes. What on earth did they
have to talk about for that long?

Finally he walked in. She hurried over to him.

"All you all right? Did they pressure you to
stay?" she asked.

He pulled her close and kissed her forehead.
"You're worried about me."

"Well, duh. What did you think? Now tell me
everything. You didn't accept the job permanently, did you?"

"What makes you think they asked?"

"It's just a matter of time until they start pressuring you. You're doing a great job. Why
wouldn't they want to keep you?"

He led her over to the sofa, then pulled her down next to him. "You're right. That's what they wanted. Helen held them off, saying they should make sure they had the right candidate. While I'm not interested in staying, at least she bought me some time." He took her hand. "She's not on my side in this. She cares about the company."

She leaned back into the leather sofa and sighed. "You don't know that."

"Actually, I do. I respect her position. If I were her, I'd do the same thing."

"But you're not her. You still want to leave."

"I *will* leave."

She looked at him. "Were they all upset?"

"They weren't happy but until the will is read, Helen controls the majority of the stock. That puts her in power." He pulled her close. "Don't kid yourself, though. If she decides she needs me to stay, she'll be the first one holding out the employment contract."

"I don't want to argue about Helen," she told him.

"Me, either." He stood and crossed to a glass cabinet by the window. After opening one of the doors, he held up an empty glass. "Want a drink?"

"No, thanks."

He poured one for himself and took a sip. "I don't know where everything went wrong with my dad and his sons."

"You probably never will. Sometimes families have trouble connecting."

"If Mom hadn't died…" He shrugged and took another sip.

She stood. There was something different about Jack. He was hurting and that pain made him vulnerable. She'd never seen him as anything but strong and powerful, so this side of him surprised her.

She crossed to him and put her arms around him. "You did the best you could."

"Maybe. Can we change the subject?"

"Sure." She gazed up into his eyes. "You were right about making us practice. It made a big difference."

He smiled and put down his drink. "I'm right about a lot of things."

"Yes, you are."

He put his arms around her and drew closer. "I was right about you and the job."

She laughed. "So we're going to make a list of all your perfections?"

"I have the time."

She glanced at the closed door. "Or we could do something else."

He raised his eyebrows. "Ms. Edwards, it's the middle of a workday."

"Yes, it is."

"Are you making advances at me?"

"Actually, I was just sort of noticing how very big your desk is. I like a big desk."

Chapter Ten

"You've sent them e-mails?" Jack asked, frustrated because he already knew the answer to the question.

"Repeatedly," Mrs. Wycliff said. "I also sent letters using overnight delivery. I know the letters were received—Evan and Andrew had to sign for them."

His brothers were ignoring his attempts to get in touch with them. He suspected they were following the financial news and knew about the trouble with the company. He had a feeling neither of them would resurface until things were better or it was time for the reading of the will—whichever came first.

Someone knocked on his open door. He glanced up and saw David standing in the doorway.

Jack excused his assistant and waved in his uncle.

"Did you hear?" he asked.

"Most of it," David said. "Evan and Andrew are still refusing to get in touch with you?"

Jack nodded. "I don't suppose either of them has contacted you and asked you not to say anything about it."

"Sorry, no."

"We haven't spoken in years," Jack said. "How the hell did that happen? When did this family get so screwed up?"

"Your mother's death didn't help."

"I was just thinking that a few days ago. If she'd been alive, so much would have been different, but with her gone it was easy to go our separate ways."

"George didn't help," David admitted. "He was more interested in the business than in his family."

Jack nodded slowly. "I remember when I was young, people would tell me I was just like him. That always scared me. I knew I loved my father, but I wasn't sure I liked him. I wanted more than that from my kids."

"You don't have any kids," his uncle reminded him.

"I noticed that, too. After Shelby…" He shook his head. No reason to go there. "I think one of the reasons may be it's the only way to make sure I don't repeat his mistakes."

"Kind of like cutting off your arm to make sure you don't get a hangnail."

"You're saying I'm taking things to the extreme."

David shrugged. "You know what your father did that you didn't like. So don't do that."

Sounded simple enough. "When I was a kid, I didn't know what I was doing that made people think I was like him, so I didn't know how to stop doing it."

"You're not a kid anymore."

"None of us are," Jack said. "I haven't talked to Evan and Andrew in years and ever since I've been working at this damn company, I miss them. Oh, sure, I want them home to do what they need to be doing. I want them to help out. But I also want to talk to them. Hang out. Like we used to. We were a family once."

"Maybe it's time to make that happen again," David said. "Maybe it's time to start pulling together instead of pulling apart."

"I'm willing. What I don't know is how to do it. I can't even get my brothers to return my e-mails. I'm ready to resort to threats."

"Might not be a bad idea. Get them back for any reason, even if it's just to protect their personal interest."

"I agree," Jack said, "but I don't like it. They're my brothers. I shouldn't have to use threats to get them to communicate with me. There has to be another way."

"I'm out of ideas," David told him.

Jack was, too, but he knew someone who might not be.

"How do I get my brothers back?" Jack asked.

Helen raised her eyebrows. "Why do you think I would know the answer to that?"

"Because I've finally figured out you know us a whole lot better than we know you. I need them here and I'll do anything to get them in Chicago."

"Even ask for my help." She smiled. "Evil stepmothers are often invisible. It can come in handy."

"I never thought you were evil."

"I know. You simply didn't think of me at all. I wasn't trying to be your mother. I just wanted to be a friend."

"I couldn't think of you as anything but my father's wife."

"His *second* wife," she said. "We all know what that means."

Had she wanted more? Had she wanted it all?

She didn't have children, he thought. And at her age, she was unlikely to have any. Had his father been the reason there weren't any little Helens running around? Maybe George would have had better luck with a second family.

She held up both her hands. "Okay, this conversation is getting out of hand. Since your dad died, I've been living on the emotional edge and if we continue like this any longer, I'm going to find myself sobbing uncontrollably. I think we'd both find that uncomfortable. So let's talk about your brothers. Who do you want to start with?"

"I'll let you pick."

She considered for a moment. "Andrew will come home for money. You're going to have to be blunt. Either he shows up or you cut him off. Cruel but effective. You might want to start by cutting off one of his credit cards so he gets the message."

"Done," Jack said. "And Evan?"

Helen sighed. "He'll come home for the reading of the will. He always wanted to be close to George and he'll be looking for closure."

"Then if Dad left him anything, it would prove Evan mattered to him?"

"Something like that."

"I hope he's not disappointed," Jack muttered.

"Me, too."

"I know you loved the old man, but he wasn't exactly father of the year."

Helen nodded slowly. "He tried, in his own flawed way. He loved you all."

"He loved the business more."

"No. He loved it differently. It was safe to let everyone know how he felt about the business. It never went away and did something he didn't approve of."

"Like his sons," Jack said.

"Some parents have trouble understanding that when a child makes a decision that the parent doesn't approve of, it's not personal. Children are their own people—they have to make their own lives."

"My father wanted me to live his life."

She smiled. "He couldn't understand that what you chose to do for your career had nothing to do with him. He's the one who gave you choices, and then he was angry with what you picked."

"So was I," Jack admitted. "It was as if he'd changed the rules partway through the game."

"He had, but he still loved you."

Jack studied the woman who had married his father. She looked different since the funeral. She'd become elegant in her sorrow.

He could see why his father had been drawn to her. The combination of brains and beauty.

"You were good to him," he said.

She smiled. "You don't actually know that."

"Yes, I do. It's there in the way you talk about him. You were more than he deserved. He got lucky when he picked you."

"Maybe I was the lucky one."

She was consistent. He would give her that.

He narrowed his gaze. "You're good at this, at listening and offering just the right amount of advice and encouragement. You should have had children of your own."

Helen stiffened slightly, which answered the question he hadn't asked.

"I, ah—"

"It was him, wasn't it? He said he didn't want to start another family."

She sighed. "It seemed like the right decision at the time."

"And now?" he asked.

"There's no going back."

He had the feeling that she hadn't asked for much in her marriage, but his father had refused her the one thing she'd really wanted.

"He was a selfish bastard."

"Don't say that. I made my choices and I loved your father. Knowing what I know now, I wouldn't change anything. He was a great man." She held up her hand. "You don't have to agree with me on that, but I know it to be true. I loved him. I will never love that way again."

There was a certainty and a power in the way she spoke. For the first time in his life, he envied his father. Not because he had any romantic feelings for Helen, but because the old man had been loved completely. Helen saw his faults and accepted them. She believed he was the great love of her life.

At one time Jack had wanted that for himself. He'd believed he'd found it with Shelby, but he'd been wrong.

"Back up," Jack said.

Samantha held in a low moan. "See, I was thinking I could go through life in Drive rather than Reverse. Sort of like letting go of the past. Don't you think that's important? To always move forward? It's a Zen thing. Or if not Zen, then something else Zen-like." She smiled brightly.

Jack looked at her. "We're talking about driving, not your life, and one isn't a metaphor for the other. You're going to have to learn to back up the car at some point, so why not now?"

She'd been afraid he was going to get all logical on her. "The Zen thing didn't move you even a little?"

"No."

"But you have to admit it was clever."

"Very clever. Now back into the parking space."

Had he always been this imperious? she thought as she carefully checked the empty parking lot.

There weren't any other cars to be seen, just ominous white lines marking parking spaces. Very small parking spaces.

"Go slowly," Jack told her. "Think about where you want the car to go, not where it is. Check for anything in the way, then back up slowly."

She wasn't sure when this had become the advanced class, but she was determined not to balk, despite nearly blinding fear.

She drew in a deep breath and looked at where she wanted the car to go. There was a tree there, spindly and gray. She briefly imagined the car's rear bumper only a foot or so from the tree, then she put the car in reverse and slowly began to back up.

"Keep your eyes on where you want to be, not where you are," he said.

"Hey, don't try to out-Zen the Zen master," she muttered, still watching the tree. She got closer and closer, then put on the brake and slipped the car into Park.

Jack grinned. "Pretty good," he said and opened his car door. "Check it out."

She jumped out and ran to the front of the car.

"It's perfect," she yelled, ignoring the slight angle of her car. "Perfect. I'm in between the lines and in the middle of the space." She tilted her head. "Almost."

Jack walked over and studied the car. She bit her lower lip. Not that she cared what he thought, except she did.

He put an arm around her. "Great job. Let's do it again."

Later that evening, Samantha showed up at his condo with salad fixings and two large slices of chocolate-chip cheesecake. As she shifted the bakery bag to her other hand so she could ring the bell, she realized she'd never been to his place before. All their rendezvous had taken place at her apartment.

"Why is that?" she asked as he opened the front door and waved her in.

"Why is what?"

She waited for his kiss before asking, "Why

haven't I been here before? Are you keeping secrets?"

"Have a look around and see for yourself," he said as he took her packages from her. "I'll open the wine."

An invitation to snoop. How often did that happen? But before she could take him up on it, Charlie came racing toward her.

She dropped down and hugged him. "How's my handsome guy?" she asked as she rubbed his ears. "Did you have fun this morning at the park?"

Charlie yipped his response, then led her into the condo.

The foyer opened onto a large living room with a to-die-for view of the lake and shoreline. To the left was a U-shaped kitchen with a high granite bar and three stools. Beyond that was a dining alcove that also looked out on the water.

"This place must be terrific during thunderstorms," she said.

"It is. Most weather looks pretty good if you're up high enough."

She took the glass of wine he offered and sipped. The color palette was typical guy—cream walls, beige furniture, black accent tables and cabinets for way too many electronics. Except for the fact that everything was new and expensive, the room reminded her a lot of what he'd had in grad school.

"Despite your fear of it," she said with a grin, "color doesn't kill. Imagine what this place would be with a red accent pillow or a bowl of green apples."

"Imagine."

Even his artwork was subdued—the two seascapes were muted and dark. There was an impressive abstract in the dining room that was mostly reds and oranges.

"This looks out of place," she said. "I'm guessing you didn't buy it."

He stared at the painting for a long time.

Samantha got a twisted feeling in her stomach. There were memories in that painting. Good or bad? she wondered, knowing there was danger in both.

"Helen gave me that when I made partner," he said quietly. "It was her way of reaching out to me. I should have seen that before, but I didn't."

Samantha studied the painting again and felt the relief sift through her. "Helen always had great taste."

He waved toward the entrance to the hallway. "Have at it."

"If you insist."

The first door on the right opened to a small powder room with a pedestal sink. Next was a home office with a television on the wall and more law books than she'd ever seen in her life. There was also a very large and squishy-looking bed for Charlie. She found a linen closet—mostly empty and painfully neat, and, last but not least, the master bedroom.

Once again beige ruled the day. A beige-and-cream bedspread covered the dark wood sleigh bed. There weren't any throw pillows, nothing decorating the nightstands. Just lamps, a clock and a TV remote.

An armoire stood opposite the bed. She would bet money that inside there was a television, because God forbid he should miss a single play of whatever sports game he was watching. More massive windows offered an incredible view, while the master bath had a steam shower and a tub big enough for two.

Gorgeous, she thought, but impersonal. There weren't any family pictures, no little items picked up on travels, no magazines lying around. No memories.

"What do you think?" he asked as he walked into the room and leaned against the door frame.

"Beautiful, but a little too beige for my taste."

"Sorry. I tried to get out and buy a throw for the bed, but time got away from me."

She laughed. "Do you even know what a throw is?"

"Sure. It's something that you, ah, throw."

"What does it look like?"

"It's brown."

She grinned. "You're hopeless."

"You should even be impressed that I could use *throw* in a sentence."

"I am."

He walked toward her and took her hand. "Come on," he said. "I'll build us a fire. We'll get wild back here later."

"I like that idea."

She curled up on the sofa while he put in kindling, then actual wood logs. Minutes later, when the fire had taken hold, he joined her on the sofa.

"Comfy?" he asked.

She nodded as she angled toward him. Then, thinking about the lack of personal touches, said, "You know all about my past, but you never talk about your own."

Nothing about his expression changed, still she sensed him pulling back a little.

"Too sensitive a topic?" she asked.

"Not for me. What do you want to know?"

"What you've been doing for the past ten years," she said, speaking honestly. "Romantically, I mean. I know all about your checkered career path."

"Checkered? I was a lawyer."

She smiled. "Exactly. Environmental law I could have understood."

"Because you have an inherent love of tree huggers."

"Absolutely. But criminal law. That's a little scary."

"Everyone deserves the chance to be defended."

She sipped her wine. "I don't actually agree

with that. Some people don't deserve anything but punishment."

"How can you know they're not innocent?"

He was being logical, one of his more annoying features. "Sometimes you just know." She sighed. "Okay, perhaps it's best I'm not in charge of our criminal justice system. Which is why you'll be a much better judge than me. But this isn't what I wanted to talk about."

"You want to know about my love life."

"Pretty much."

He shrugged. "Shelby's the most significant relationship and you know about her."

That she'd died. "That must have been so horrible."

"It wasn't fun. After her, I didn't date for a long time."

"Because you were still in love with her?"

His mouth straightened, which didn't tell her all that much about what he was thinking. She tried to read the emotions in his eyes, but they flashed by too quickly.

"I'm not sure it was love as much as I didn't want to answer questions. I never knew when to tell someone I was dating that my fiancée had been killed shortly before the wedding. Too soon and it looked like I was fishing for sympathy. Too late and I was accused of keeping secrets. It was easier not to get involved at all."

Which all sounded reasonable, she thought, but she didn't buy into it. He didn't date because it was too hard to explain his past? Maybe for someone else, but not Jack. He was used to thinking on his feet. As for making a convincing argument, it was what he did for a living.

"So you avoided relationships?" she asked.

"Serious ones. I've fallen into a pattern of serial monogamy and it's working for me."

"Don't you get lonely and want more?" She held up her free hand. "I'm asking intellectually. I'm not fishing."

"You mean love and happily-ever-after." He shook his head. "I'm not a big believer in that. Are you?"

"I shouldn't be," she said slowly. "What with my divorce and all. But I know love exists. I loved Vance, at least at first. Helen loved George."

"Maybe it's something women are good at," Jack said.

"Meaning men aren't? There's an abdication of responsibility."

"I don't know a whole lot of guys who are in happy relationships. Did my father really love Helen? I hope so, for her sake. But from what I saw about the old man, it seems unlikely. My brothers have sure stayed away from anything serious. Even David, who is the most normal, centered guy I know, has managed to avoid marriage."

"Are you saying it's a bad deal for men?"

"No. I'm not advocating that guys need to screw around. I don't know how anyone gives with his or her whole heart. How do you take that step of faith? In my world, people you love leave."

"Including Shelby?"

"Especially Shelby."

But his fiancée had died, Samantha thought. Was it fair to blame her for something that wasn't her fault?

"Is that why there aren't any pictures of her around?" she asked. "Because you're angry with her?"

"I stopped being angry a long time ago. It's not about anger. It's about letting go."

She took another sip of her wine and sighed. "It's funny—I'm fighting you on your theory about giving it all and truly falling in love when I know Vance didn't love me. Not the way I loved him. I don't know what he felt. If you were to ask him, he would swear he loved me. He would talk about all the ways he proved it. But that wasn't love."

"What was it?"

She didn't mean to say anything. The word just sort of slipped out. "Control."

Jack raised his eyebrows, but didn't speak. She found herself filling the silence.

"He wasn't like that before we got married. At least not so much. He might make a suggestion about something I was wearing, or what I planned to cook for dinner. I thought he was interested. I thought it was a good thing."

"It wasn't?"

"No. He began to monitor my life. How much time I spent at work, how long it took me to get home. He wouldn't let me wear certain things. He said they were too sexy. He accused me of being interested in a couple of guys at work, which was crazy. I wasn't interested in anyone. Then he started telling me it didn't matter because no one…"

She swallowed. Okay, how had she gotten into *this* conversation. Big mistake.

"Because no one what?" Jack asked.

She stared at her lap. "Because no one else would want me. He said I was lucky he wanted me."

"He abused you." Jack's words were flat.

She looked at him. "He didn't hit me." She made a harsh sound that was supposed to be close to a laugh. "Isn't that horrible? I told myself that for more than two years. He wasn't hitting me so it couldn't be abuse. He was just tired, or I'd made him angry. But he would scream at me and make me feel useless and small. I told myself I was letting it happen, because no one can make you feel anything if you don't let them, right? So there was something wrong with me. But I didn't know how to fix it and Vance was always there, in my face, speaking my worst fears."

She felt the tension in Jack and didn't want to know what he was thinking. Just talking about her past made her feel small and ashamed.

"I was a fool," she said quietly. "I equated attention with love. Vance was attentive. Too attentive. He separated me from my friends, my mom, he didn't like me spending long hours at work. I saw what I had become and I hated it. But I didn't know how to make it better."

"You left," he said.

She nodded. "I can't even tell you what happened. One day I came home and he was complaining about my clothes and my body and telling me I was stupid and I just snapped. I threw a vase at him. It hit him in the chest, then dropped to the floor. He screamed louder, saying I was in trouble now. It was like he was my father and I was his child. I suddenly realized I didn't have to be there. So I left."

Jack didn't say anything, but she could hear him thinking.

"You're judging me," she said, feeling defensive and vulnerable.

"No. You got out. That takes courage."

All the right words, but why was he staring at her as if she were a bug? "But?" she asked.

"I'm surprised it happened at all. You're strong and powerful. I wouldn't have thought a guy like that could mess with you."

"You're saying I should have seen it coming."

"No. Why would you? You trusted this guy. Any signs would have been…"

"Signs?"

He shifted uncomfortably. "No one changes overnight."

"I see. So you think I missed big clues. That I'm as much to blame?"

"No. Not to blame. If you'd never been in the situation before, you couldn't have known. You got out. You fought."

She stood. She hated this. Hated what had happened, hated telling him. She felt exposed and flawed. Unworthy.

"We can't all make perfect decisions," she said, trying not to get angry, knowing her temper was a defense mechanism. "I screwed up with Vance. While it was happening, I kept wondering what I'd done wrong. Was I listening to my mother? Subconsciously trying to keep a rich powerful guy around so I would be safe? Only I wasn't safe. And if I knew that, why was leaving so hard? That's what I hate. How hard it was to go. How long it took me. I'm sure this is all too confusing for you. Your world is simply black and white. You don't get involved. You don't risk anything. That does make things simpler, doesn't it?"

"Samantha." He stood and moved toward her.

She flinched, then put her wine on the coffee table. "This wasn't a good idea. I need to go."

"Wait. We should talk."

Suddenly, she couldn't. The past was there, pressing down on her. He was wrong—Vance *had* changed so completely. There had been no warning. Vance had been so much like Jack.

She hurried out of the condo and ran for the

elevator. Jack followed. The doors opened and she slipped inside.

"Samantha, wait."

But she didn't and when she got back to her apartment, he didn't bother to come after her.

Chapter Eleven

Jack had no idea what had gone wrong with Samantha. He mentally went over their conversation several times and still wasn't sure where they'd derailed. What had he said to upset her? Did she think he wasn't impressed she'd gotten away? A lot of women didn't. There were several cases in his law office, abusive husbands who had murdered their wives. Those women hadn't been able to get away, but Samantha had.

He clicked on another computer file, hoping work would distract him. Unfortunately, it didn't. He kept seeing the hurt in Samantha's eyes, the pain as she ran from him, as if he were just like Vance.

Vance. Is that where he'd gone wrong, saying that there had to be signs? He believed that was true. Maybe Samantha hadn't seen them, but he, Jack, was willing to bet that there had been clues.

Not that he would say that to Samantha now. He doubted she wanted to speak with him about anything personal. He hadn't heard from her in a couple of days and he sure as hell didn't know how to open the lines of communication.

Under normal circumstances, he would simply accept that the relationship had unworkable flaws and move on. He'd told himself to do that just this morning. The only problem was he didn't want to move on. He wanted to know that Samantha was okay. He wanted to explain that he'd never meant to hurt her, and then he wanted to find a way to make it all right between them.

Yeah, right—because he had so much success

in his personal relationships. Based on his track record, Samantha should stay as far away from him as possible.

He glanced at his watch and groaned. The last full staff meeting before the Web site launch was due to start in ten minutes. So he was going to have his desired chance to speak with Samantha. Unfortunately, it would be in front of her entire team and the IT guys.

He collected his notes and walked to the main conference room. Samantha and her people were already there, setting up for their Power-Point presentation. Jack nodded and took a seat at the conference table, doing his best not to notice how feminine and sexy she looked in her loose, flowing blouse and long skirt.

"Morning," Samantha said, her smile bright, but still not reaching her eyes. "We're on schedule with everything. If you'll just give us a minute to get a few last minute glitches out of the flowcharts, we'll be good to go."

"Take your time," Jack told her.

Arnie burst into the room and hurried to her side. After an intense, whispered conversation, Arnie handed over a memory stick, then grinned and took the seat next to Jack's.

"Hey," the younger man said. "Pretty exciting stuff, huh? We've been working day and night to get the Web site ready to launch. Some of the interactive links are going to blow everyone away."

"That's what we're looking for," Jack said as Roger walked into the room.

Arnie's boss sat across from Jack.

"Morning," Jack said.

Roger nodded, not looking happy. "This has all been rushed through," Roger said. "I hope we can meet the deadline."

Jack looked at Arnie, who shifted uncomfortably in his seat. "We'll get there, boss. You'll see."

Jack knew that the Web site wasn't Roger's

idea of a good time. What he didn't understand was how someone could get to be the head of the IT department and not be interested in innovation.

Samantha stepped in front of the conference table. "All right, we're ready. Welcome to the new and improved Hanson Media Group interactive Web site for children. Today I'm going to give you a detailed look at the Web site—what's available, what's new, what we can expect to launch over the next six months. If you'll please direct your attention to the large screen on the wall, I'll begin."

Over the next ninety minutes, she outlined the Web site. Jack took a few notes, but mostly he divided his attention between the screen and Samantha.

She spoke with the confidence of someone who knew her material and believed in what she was doing. She fielded questions and offered opinions. When the discussion got too technical, she handed control over to Arnie, who explained things to the point where Jack was lost in a sea of computer terms.

When they'd finished, Samantha invited them all to the launch party Wednesday afternoon, when the site went live.

Everyone rose. Jack lingered until he and Samantha were the last two in the room.

"Good job," he said. "Arnie's worked out well for you."

She nodded. "He's been great. He's not only good at the technical stuff, but he understands the creative process. He's a big fan of yours and your dad's. He talks about George all the time. How George was really there for him."

"Good to know," Jack said. "Think he would be interested in running the department?"

She frowned. "Why do you want my opinion?"

"You've worked with him. You know how he thinks, what he's like. Could he do the job?"

"I think so. You're going to fire Roger?"

Jack sighed. "I don't know. I'm going to talk

to him about his attitude. If he can't get onboard with what we're doing, then yes. It's never my first choice, but sometimes it has to be done. Given that, I would prefer to promote from within."

"Arnie's really popular with the IT team. That can be both good and bad. He might not enjoy the transition from one of the guys to being in charge."

"Once I decide what I'm doing with Roger, I'll talk with Arnie," Jack said. "I appreciate your candor."

She smiled. "No problem. As you know, I have opinions on nearly everything. Anything else you want to know about?"

What went wrong between the two of them, he thought, but before he could ask, she collected her files and computer.

"Never mind," she said quickly. "I have another meeting."

And then she was gone.

She'd always done that, he reminded himself. Disappeared when the going got tough. Ten years ago, when he'd pushed for more, she'd resisted and then she'd retreated. She proved his point about people leaving.

So he should just forget about her. It was the intelligent thing to do. And he would. Just as soon as he figured out how to get her out of his head…and his heart.

"So what exactly is the problem?" Helen asked.

Samantha writhed on the cream-colored sofa and covered her face with her hands. "Nothing."

"Of course I believe you, what with how calmly you're acting."

"It's crazy. It's dumb."

Her friend curled up in the club chair opposite and tucked her feet under herself. "You screwed up."

Samantha looked at her. "Do you have to be so blunt?"

"It seems called for. What's the problem? Did you blow it with Jack? I know it's not work related. I've only been hearing good things about you in that respect."

"Really? What kind of things?"

"They would not be the point of this conversation. What happened?"

Samantha flopped down on the sofa and groaned. "I blew it. Seriously. I'm going to be a cautionary tale."

Helen waited expectantly but didn't speak.

Samantha groaned. "Fine, I'll tell you, but it's not pretty."

She detailed the conversation she'd had with Jack at his place a few days ago.

"I freaked," she admitted after she'd shared the specifics. "He didn't really say anything that bad, it was all me. I felt guilty and embarrassed and stupid. As if I'd disappointed him somehow. As if it were my fault. I didn't like feeling that way. I didn't know how to deal with it so I overreacted. Worse, I blamed him."

"Actually, I think the worse part is that you walked out without explaining."

Samantha raised her head and glared at her friend. "You're not being helpful."

"Of course I am. I'm telling you the truth. The problem isn't that Jack couldn't handle the past, it's that you still can't. You don't want to believe you were that stupid." Helen smiled. "I'm saying this with love. You know that, right?"

"Yes. I feel the love. Sort of. It's me. It's all me. I'm ashamed and I feel like an idiot. I'm strong and tough, just like Jack said. How did I let some guy abuse me? How did I let him cut me off from my support system? Why couldn't I see the signs?"

"Because you weren't looking for them. You took Vance at his word. That's not exactly a crime."

"Maybe not, but it turned out to be poor judgment on my part. I feel horrible."

"I'm not the one you should be sharing your feelings with."

Samantha rolled onto her side. "You're saying I need to go talk to Jack."

"I can't think of another way to fix the situation."

"But what if he hates me?"

"Gee, what if you stopped being so dramatic?"

Samantha grinned. "Okay. Hate is strong. What if…" She sat up. "What if he doesn't respect me anymore?"

"What if he does? There's only one way to find out what he's thinking and that's to ask him."

Samantha knew her friend was telling the truth. "So when do I get to be the mature one in the relationship?"

"Next time."

"Ha. Like I believe that. You're so good at this. I guess it's because you had a great marriage. I want that. I want someone to love me and care about me, all the while seeing me as an equal."

"If you really want it, it will happen."

"Sort of like if you build it, they will come?"

"Yes, but this time in a romantic sense. If you know what you want, it's within your grasp."

Meaning Jack. Did she want him? Them?

"We're doing the serial monogamy thing," she said. "Nothing long term."

"Okay, then after Jack."

After. Right. Because what were the odds of finding someone better than him? Someone more honest and funny and charming and better in bed?

"He doesn't want more," Samantha said. "He told me so."

"Do you know why?"

"Sort of. He doesn't believe people stay."

"A lot of people have left him, including you."

"I don't want to think about that."

"Maybe it's time you should," Helen said. "Why did you go?"

"Because I thought he'd hurt me. I thought he was too much like my father. But he's not. Although Vance was. This is confusing."

"What do you know for sure?"

"That I have to tell Jack I'm sorry."

Helen smiled. "Want me to show you out?"

Jack was home and he answered the door right away. Samantha had been hoping for a bit more time to figure out what she was going to say to him.

"Hi," he said and stepped back. "Want to come in?"

Just like that. No recriminations, no questions as to whether or not she was going to bite off his head.

"Thanks. Is this a good time?" she asked as she moved into the foyer and looked around for Charlie. Dogs were always a good distraction.

"Sure. What did you have in mind?"

He looked so good that she wanted to skip the conversation and suggest they move into the bedroom. He'd pulled on a sweater over worn jeans and pushed up the sleeves. He wore socks, but no shoes and had that weary end-of-the-day stubble that made her want to rub her hands against his jaw.

"I have a couple of things I'd like to say," she told him instead, not because it was the mature thing, and therefore the most Helen-like, but because she had a bad feeling he wouldn't be interested in sleeping with her right now.

Charlie came strolling down the hall, his yawn betraying his most recent activity.

"Did you just get up?" she asked the dog as she bent over and rubbed his ears.

"He had a tough day at doggy day care," Jack told her. "Apparently he played until he dropped from exhaustion."

That's right. Big tough ol' Jack took his

dog to day care. How was she supposed to resist that?

"Come on," he said, leading the way into the living room. "Have a seat."

"Okay." She followed him, then perched on the edge of the seat cushion. "I just wanted to apologize for what happened the last time I was here. I kind of lost it."

He sat at the other end of the sofa and faced her. "You seemed upset."

"I was. And hurt and embarrassed. I sort of took all that out on you." Wait. There was no *sort of.* "I *did* take that out on you. I thought you were judging me."

"Samantha, I wasn't," he told her. "Never that."

"I figured that part out later. By then I was home and giving myself a stern talking-to. The thing is, I'm not proud of what happened with Vance. I still don't know how I let him take control of me, of the situation. I've tried to learn from what happened. The control thing started so small. With little tiny suggestions. They grew and before I knew it…"

She shrugged. "My point is, it was my problem. Your comment about seeing clues was valid."

"Maybe, but it was poorly timed," he admitted. "It's a guy thing—wanting to fix. I know better."

"You didn't do anything wrong. I just hated believing you think badly of me."

"Not that." He moved close and took her hands in his. "Never that. I admire what you did. You found yourself in a hellish situation and you got out. You fought. Shelby didn't."

What? "What does your late fiancée have to do with my poor judgment with men?"

He released her hands and stood. "I told you Shelby died shortly before our wedding, but there's more to it than that. She'd been depressed for a while. Looking back, I suspect she'd been depressed all her life. We met during one of the times when she was feeling good. It didn't last." He walked to the window and stared out at the city.

"I didn't understand what was happening," he admitted. "She would get so sad and withdrawn. It was almost as if she disappeared from life. I thought it was me. I thought I was doing something wrong. But then the depression would ease and we'd be fine. She started seeing a therapist and she put her on medication. It helped. For a while. That's when I proposed. I figured this was just a manageable disease, like diabetes. I was wrong."

Samantha didn't know what to think. Jack was so vibrant and full of life. She couldn't imagine him with someone who was too depressed to deal with the world.

"Planning the wedding was too much," he said, his back to her. "I figured that out too late to do anything. Her mother tried to help. Helen offered, but I wasn't willing to deal with her. We had a bad storm and Shelby went driving in it. She lost control. At least that's what the police said. It was an accident."

Samantha couldn't breathe. Her heart ached for him. "It wasn't, was it?" she asked with a gasp.

He shook his head. "She left me a note. I burned it as soon as I read it. I knew the truth would only hurt her parents. They thought she was doing better, that she was finally happy. They actually thanked me for that at the funeral."

He turned to look at her. "I knew it was better to let them think what they wanted. Why hurt them after she was gone? Why tell them she would rather be dead than married to me?"

Samantha sprang to her feet and hurried to him. "Is that what you think? It's not true, Jack. Don't you see? She was sick. You were right to call what she had a disease. Blaming yourself for her depression is as crazy as blaming me for Vance's abuse. You were there for her. You tried to help. In the end, she couldn't handle life and that has nothing to do with you."

She touched his arms, his back, trying to make him see. "You have to believe me," she whispered.

"I want to. You don't know how much. It's been a long time and I've let it go. But every now and then I wonder what I could have done differently. How I could have saved her."

"You can't save someone who won't save herself."

He turned then, and looked at her. "You saved yourself. That's what I was thinking the other night. You saved yourself."

They stared at each other. All their polite pretenses and shields were down. There was only the moment and the raw pain swirling around them, taking them to a level of emotional intimacy that was so real, so deep, it hurt.

Her first instinct was to run. If she stayed, if she let him in and they dealt with this together, there might not be an escape. She might start to care too much. She might get lost inside of him.

But there was no denying the truth. That they'd each shared their most intimate secret. They knew the worst about each other. So where did they go from here?

He must have read the question in her eyes, because he answered it by grabbing her, pulling her in close and kissing her. She responded by surging toward him, silently begging for more.

He wrapped his arms around her as if he would never let her go. She welcomed the heat and power of his embrace. He was not a tentative lover—he claimed with a forceful need that took her breath away. Right now she had to know he wanted her, she had to know this mattered, and he told her over and over again as his mouth claimed hers in a kiss that touched her soul.

Wanting grew as she tasted him and felt her body sigh and swell and dampen. She ran her hands up and down his back, then across his broad shoulders. His strength excited her. She loved the feel of his muscles bunching and releasing. When he dropped his hands to her hips and urged her closer, she arched toward him and felt the satisfying hardness of his desire.

"More," she breathed.

He took her at her word and raised his hands to her breasts. He cupped her slight curves, teasing the sensitive skin before lightly brushing her hard nipples. Pleasure shot through her. She gasped, then let her head drop back as she lost herself in the tingling, burning, arousing sensation of his gentle touch.

Over and over he teased her, rubbing her breasts, stroking her. Even through the layers of her blouse and her bra, the feelings were exquisite. He leaned in and kissed the side of her neck, then gently bit down on her bare skin.

She shuddered in anticipation of them making love. Her brain filled with images of them naked, reaching, surging, claiming. Suddenly she needed him naked and inside of her. She stepped back and reached for his clothes.

"Now," she commanded.

Either he wanted the same thing, or he understood exactly what she needed. He reached for her blouse as she reached for his sweater. Their arms bumped and it probably would have made more sense for them to each undress themselves, but she didn't want that. She wanted to be the one to reveal his warm, naked flesh. She wanted to undo his belt, push down his jeans and briefs and reach for him, even as he jerked her skirt and panties to her ankles.

She stepped out of both, along with her clogs. Then they were naked and reaching and they were touching everywhere. Even as he kissed her deeply, thrusting his tongue into her mouth, he reached for her bare breasts. She ran her hands down his back, pausing when she reached his butt. Once there, she caressed the high, tight curve, then squeezed.

His arousal flexed against her stomach. So hard,

she thought, loving how much he wanted her. She was already wet—she ached with readiness.

Once again, he seemed to read her mind. He pushed her back until she felt the sofa behind her. They dropped onto the cool, soft surface, a tangle of arms and legs and need. He shifted her until she sprawled across the cushions, her legs parted, her body exposed. He slid onto the floor, then bent forward, bringing his mouth into contact with her most intimate spot.

Samantha surrendered to the magic of his tongue and lips as he explored every sensitive inch of her. He licked her thoroughly before focusing his attention on that single spot of pleasure. Even as she felt herself both melting and tensing as she strained toward her completion, he slipped a finger inside of her.

The combination was too much for her to stand. Her breath quickened as her muscles clenched. Her climax became a certainty so all she had to do was simply brace herself for the explosion.

When it crashed into her, she gasped her pleasure. Her body contracted and stiffened, only to become boneless. Still he moved in and out, while kissing and licking and circling. As long as he touched her, she came—again and again. The orgasm stretched out until every cell in her body sighed in delight.

At last he slowed and her contractions eased. When he raised his head and looked at her, she found herself feeling more exposed than she ever had. Raw emotion made her uncomfortable. But she was trapped and naked and there was no escape.

Then Jack smiled. "You're so incredible," he murmured. "So beautiful. I could do that for hours."

With a few simple words, he made her feel special and at ease. She opened her arms and welcomed him. He moved close, shifting so that he could slide his arousal into her waiting warmth. Her body tensed slightly and he groaned.

He put his hands on her hips and drew her closer, then he shifted one hand so he could touch her breast. She wrapped her legs around his hips, urging him deeper and deeper, wanting to get lost in him, as he was lost in her.

She felt him harden, stiffen, then still. His release claimed him. She kept her eyes open and watched his face tighten. At the last possible moment, he opened his eyes as well and they stared at each other.

It was a perfect moment of connection, she thought in wonder. She was truly one with this man. And in love with him.

The revelation stunned her but, once admitted, the truth wouldn't go away.

She loved Jack.

She didn't know if the feeling was new or if it had been in hiding for the past ten years, but she loved him and she didn't have a clue as to what she was going to do about it.

Chapter Twelve

"We have plans, Jack," Harold Morrison said as he handed a glass of scotch to Jack's boss.

Jack held his drink until everyone was served, then waited for the toast.

"To men who have the potential to go places," Morrison said.

Everyone glanced at Jack. He nodded, rather than smiled. "I appreciate the support and encouragement," he said before taking a drink.

"We think you can make it all the way,"

Morrison told him. "We've been talking about you."

Jack glanced around at the ten other people in the room. There were the four senior partners from his law firm, two congressmen, the junior senator and three officials from the state party office. Six men and four women, all of whom had the power to influence his future.

Morrison patted Jack on the back. "You need to get things squared away at Hanson Media Group. You're doing a good job. We're getting excellent reports. Sure, you're not practicing law, but you're being a leader, making decisions. That bodes well. Just don't screw up there."

Everyone laughed but Jack.

"You'll be back at the law firm in another couple of months," Morrison continued. "Once that happens, you'll be put on the short list for an appointment to the circuit court as an associate judge. The law firms like to send good people into the judicial system. It makes us look good."

More laughter.

"I'll do my best," Jack said, knowing there was little he could do to move the process along. The launch of the Web site was only days away. Once that was up and running and adding to the cash flow, he could focus his attention on the many other problems. Two months, Morrison had said. Was it enough time?

Jack knew that legally he could walk away any time he wanted. Without signing a permanent contract with the board, they couldn't stop him from leaving. But legal obligations were different than moral ones. Hanson Media Group was the family company. Could he turn his back on it and let it fail so he'd be free to pursue his own dreams?

It was a question he had yet to answer.

Sarah Johnson, one of the firm's senior

partners, leaned her hip on the conference-room table. "After working as an appointed judge, you'll run as an elected one. We'll have an organization in place to help with that. We've seen how you think and we like what we see. You're fair without being sentimental and you consider all your options. That's good for everyone. If you do as well as we expect, it won't be long until you're appointed to the federal bench." She raised her glass. "I like the sound of that."

"Agreed," Jack said, then took a sip of his drink. Big plans. Why did it have to come down to a choice between doing what he wanted and doing what was right for a family business he didn't care about?

"Was it wonderful?" Samantha asked as she walked into Jack's office for their quick lunch together.

"It's the first time I've had liquor before

noon." He frowned as he thought about college. "At least in a lot of years."

"Oooh, you were drinking. That's good, right?"

"I'm not sure the drinking mattered, but there was a spirit of celebration."

She moved toward him and smiled. "I like the sound of that," she said as she raised herself on tiptoes and lightly brushed his mouth with hers. "They're impressed with you—just like me."

As always, her closeness made him aware of his ever-present need for her. It didn't seem to matter how many times they made love, the wanting wouldn't go away.

She set a tote bag on the coffee table and sank onto the sofa. After pulling out two wrapped sandwiches, she held one in each hand.

"Turkey or ham?" she asked.

"Either."

She passed him the ham, then dug around for take-out cartons of salad, two bags of chips and napkins. He took two sodas out of the small refrigerator in the corner and settled next to her on the sofa.

"There's a plan in place," he said as he unwrapped his sandwich. "I have the support of the senior partners, along with a couple of guys from congress and our junior senator."

"That's great," she said. "Did you get to meet them?"

He nodded. "They said they like the way I think. Plus having a former member of a law firm moving up the judicial food chain is always good for getting clients."

She frowned. "Because they think they'll get a break in cases?"

He smiled for the first time that morning. "No. Because it means they can pick and groom talent. Any sign that I was favoring one side over another in a case would mean getting thrown off the bench. I haven't busted my butt to get this far only to screw up over something that stupid."

"Okay. That makes sense. So if you look good, they look good."

"Yeah. There's only one thing standing in the way of all that."

She tilted her head. "I don't even have to guess. What are you going to do?"

"I haven't decided. Part of me wants to call a board meeting and resign. What do I care about this company?"

She touched his hand. "Except you do care. You don't want all the employees to be out of a job and there's a tiny part of you that can't face losing the company your father loved so much."

He stiffened. "I don't give a damn about my father." Why would he?

But instead of backing off, Samantha stayed exactly where she was and took a bite of her sandwich. The silence lengthened. Finally he exhaled sharply.

"Fine. I might not care about the old man, but

you're right. I can't let this all be destroyed. It would be wrong."

She swallowed, then smiled. "Why was I afraid of you back in grad school? I kept seeing you as exactly like my father, but you couldn't be more different."

"Why were you afraid of me?"

"Because I thought you'd hurt me, then leave me."

Instead she'd been the one to walk out, he thought. "I'm not like him or Vance," he said.

"I know that now."

Better late than never, or was it? In the ten years they'd been apart, they'd both learned lessons. Unfortunately, his had been to be wary of trusting anyone to stay.

"I want to talk to Helen," she said. "About getting you back to your law firm. She can take on the board, she's good at that kind of stuff. There has to be someone else who can run things around here."

He leaned close and lightly touched her face. "Not your concern."

"I want you to have your heart's desire. Why wouldn't I?"

Very few people bothered to look out for him these days, he thought. David had when he'd been younger. Now Samantha was stepping into his life and doing her best to make his dreams come true.

"Why does it matter?" he asked, when what he really meant was "Why do *I* matter?"

She smiled. "It just does." She pushed his sandwich toward him. "You'd better eat. Mrs. Wycliff said you had a full afternoon."

He unwrapped the paper and took a bite, but his mind was busy elsewhere. Her words, her actions, all spoke of caring about him. He'd wanted that for a long, long time. Was it finally happening? Could he trust her not to bolt? And if she was willing to stick around this time, was he willing to open himself up or had he been burned one too many times?

"I'm going to throw up," Samantha muttered, doing her best to stay calm and keep breathing.

Arnie hovered at her side. "You'll be fine. We're all fine."

She laughed. "You look like you're going to pass out. That's hardly fine." Her humor faded. "Jeez, I hate this. Why can't it be tomorrow? Why can't the launch be behind us?"

"Because it's now."

And it was. She stood in the corner of an after-school center in the middle of the city. The large computer lab was filled with excited kids, members of the media and most of her team and the IT staff.

Dozens of conversations competed with laughter and loud music. There were bright balloons, plush toys licensed from animation on the Web site and a cake big enough to feed a hometown Bears crowd.

They had been live for all of eighteen minutes and she was still scared to go see how it was going.

"It's my job," she muttered to herself and took a step toward the computers.

"What do you think?" she asked the boy sitting closest to her.

He was maybe eleven, with bright red hair and freckles. "It's fun. I can do my math homework and get help when I need it. Plus, there's this game."

He clicked on several icons faster than she could follow and ended up in a math-based jungle where three different paths offered three different games.

Samantha made a few notes and then moved on to another child. About a half hour later, David Hanson strolled up and said, "You can't hide from the media forever," he said. "They have questions."

"I'm nervous," she admitted.

"It doesn't show. Come on. It won't be so bad."

Samantha followed him to the row of reporters and newspeople. David introduced her.

"We'll start with general questions," he said, "then we can schedule individual interviews and tape segments for the local news."

A pretty woman in a tailored navy suit jacket grinned. "I'm actually the network feed. This is going national."

"That's great," Samantha said, knowing it was amazing publicity and ignoring the sudden aerial formation of butterflies in her stomach. "Ask away."

She fielded several questions about how the new Web site worked.

"What about security?" one of the reporters asked. "How are you protecting our children?"

"In every way possible," Samantha told her.

"We have all the usual safeguards in place, along with specific security triggers to flag potential stalkers. There's a special section for parents on the Web site. They can set up parameters, determining how much access each child in the family has. Older kids can do more, younger kids less. We're interested in feedback on the issue as well." She smiled. "I have the time logs in my office. On this project, we've spent as many hours on security as we have on content and we're very proud of that."

The next few questions were for the director of the after-school program. Samantha took the time away from the spotlight to look around and enjoy the success. She'd had the idea of making this a reality and now it was.

"We also owe a specific debt of gratitude to Hanson Media Group," the director was saying. "Not just for the wonderful Web site, but also for the new computers and high-speed Internet access they've donated to our center."

Samantha joined in the applause, but she didn't know what the woman was talking about. As soon as the media interviews were over, she found David.

"The company donated computers to the center?" she asked.

David nodded. "It was Jack's idea. He didn't think it was right to use them to get publicity without giving something back. Their computers were pretty old."

She glanced at the man in question and saw him sitting in front of a monitor with a little girl on his lap. Two more girls leaned against him, all raptly intent on the screen.

"The donation isn't mentioned in the PR material," she said. "I reviewed it last night."

David shrugged. "Jack didn't want to exploit the moment. I told him he was crazy, but he didn't listen. He's stubborn that way."

She knew he hadn't done it for her. In fact, she was confident she'd never crossed his mind.

He'd quietly given thousands of dollars worth of computers because it was the right thing to do. That was simply the kind of man he was.

She'd let him walk out of her life once because she'd been afraid....

But not of him, she suddenly realized. Her fears had never been about him. They'd been about herself. About how she would react. About how her world would change. She'd been afraid of depending on someone who would let her down and that she wouldn't be able to handle it.

Ten years ago she'd let Jack go, not because of who he was, but because of who *she* was.

She walked toward him and as she got closer, her chest tightened. There he sat with those girls, typing in what they told him to, patiently exploring the site with them. One of the girls pointed at a colorful animated parrot and laughed. Jack smiled at the child and nodded.

Samantha got it then—she saw it all. The

acceptance, the caring, the goodness of the man inside.

She'd always wanted children. She'd put her dreams on hold because of her marriage to Vance. She'd lost so much time, but she'd been given a second chance. Was she going to blow it again? Or was she going to reach for the happiness waiting there, well within her grasp?

Friday night the Web site flashed with bright colors. The man at the keyboard typed furiously. This was wrong. All wrong. George wouldn't have wanted this. George would have wanted things to stay the same. He never approved of all this new technology.

It was the wrong direction for the company. How many times had George said Hanson Media Group was about magazines? Not this. Never this.

It was all going so well, too. Jack would get the credit. Jack who had never cared about his father.

Jack who had broken his father's heart by refusing to go into the family business. The board and everyone else would say Jack was the hero.

He typed more quickly, working links into the software programming, putting them in places no one would think to look. Because they *would* look. The IT people always wanted to fix the problem themselves.

What they would forget was that he was better than all of them. The more they dug, the farther away they would get from the actual problem.

He tested the links, then smiled. All done. Now all he had to do was crash the system. The techs on duty would work frantically to get it up and running again. When they did, they would see everything working fine. What they wouldn't see was that the Web site automatically linked to a porn site. They wouldn't know there was even another problem to deal with until it was too late.

That should punish Jack. That should punish all of them.

* * *

A fire crackled behind the grate. Jack felt the warmth on his legs, but only barely. He was far more interested in getting Samantha's bra off. But she wasn't cooperating.

"I want you naked," he murmured against her mouth.

She laughed and kissed him. "Do you see me protesting?"

"You're trying to get my shirt off. Bra first, shirt second."

"But I want to see you," she said. "You look good naked."

"See later. I want to touch now."

She smiled. "Touching is good. I would support touching."

He stared into her eyes and found himself wanting to get lost there. This is how it was supposed to be, he thought. This is what mattered. Being with someone he cared about. Someone he could trust.

A voice in his head warned him that Samantha had run before and she would probably run again, but he didn't want to listen. He didn't want to think about her leaving. Not now.

But what to say to convince her to stay? After all, he wasn't one who truly believed in relationships working out. They certainly never had for him. Was this time different?

Maybe the difference was this time he wanted it to, he thought as he bent down and kissed her.

She parted for him and he stroked her tongue with his. He tilted his head so he could deepen the kiss, then claimed her with a passion that seared him to his soul.

"Samantha," he breathed as he rolled onto his back and pulled her with him.

She draped across his chest, her body warm and yielding. Her hands were everywhere, touching, pulling at clothes, teasing and exciting. She shifted so she could rub herself against his arousal.

The sharp sound of the phone cut through the night.

He swore and considered not answering it. It was after eleven on Saturday night—what could be that important? Only an emergency, he thought grimly as Samantha sat up and handed him the phone.

"Hello?"

"Jack? Is that you? Are you watching the news?"

"What? Who is this?" Then he recognized the frantic voice. "Mrs. Wycliff?"

"Turn on the news. Any channel. It's on all of them. Oh, Jack, it's horrible. This is the end. I don't see how the company can survive now."

He grabbed the remote and turned on the television. The local late-night news anchor appeared and behind her was a screen showing a raunchy porn site. Certain body parts were blacked out, but it was easy to see what the people on the screen were doing.

Jack swore and increased the volume.

"No one from Hanson Media Group was immediately available for comment," the news anchor said. "From our best guess, the new Web site for children has been linking to this porn site for the better part of the afternoon. Parents across the country are furious and no one knows exactly how many children were exposed to this sort of smut."

Chapter Thirteen

"It's been twelve hours," Jack said, more than ready to yell at the people assembled in his office.

Most of Samantha's team was in place, as were the IT guys, along with David and Mrs. Wycliff. Although he hadn't told his secretary to come in, she'd been waiting when he'd arrived.

"Twelve goddamn hours since the site crashed and no one—*no one*—thought to call me?"

His words echoed in the large room, followed by an uncomfortable silence. Right now he didn't care about anyone being uncomfortable. He wanted answers.

"Everyone has my home number," he continued. "I've told you all to get in touch if there's a problem and the only reason I know now is because Mrs. Wycliff watched the late news. How long would this have gone on otherwise? When exactly did you plan on letting me know?"

He directed the last question at the IT staff. Roger stepped forward.

"The site crashed yesterday morning. We're not sure why. I have a team investigating. They had the site up and running in about two hours."

"At a porn site?" Jack asked sarcastically. "Wouldn't it have been better to wait until our content was available?"

Roger swallowed. "Our content is available. But when our Web address is typed in, users were redirected to the porn site you heard about. Our Web site is fine."

Jack narrowed his gaze. "I don't think I'd use

that word to describe things right now." He turned to Arnie. "Did you pull the plug?"

The smaller man nodded quickly. "Yes. As soon as I heard, I came right in. When you type in the Web address, the user gets an error message."

That was something, Jack thought grimly. At least no more children would be sent to view raunchy sex.

"Do we know what happened?" Jack asked in a quiet voice. "Do we know what went wrong?"

No one answered.

He leaned against the edge of his desk. "How bad?" he asked David.

"It's too soon to tell. We have to figure out how many hits we had this afternoon. With the publicity blitz all week, we were expecting a couple million."

Jack swore. A couple million? Was that possible? Was this company really responsible for exposing two million children to that kind of horror?

"We were supposed to be helping them," he said. "We were supposed to be providing a safe environment for children. A place where they could learn and have fun, away from everything bad. Instead we sent them right into the heart of the worst of it."

"Our stock might take a hit, but it will recover," someone said.

Jack stared at the man, not sure what department he belonged in and knowing it would be unreasonable to fire him for expressing an opinion.

"You think I care about the stock price?" he asked. "Do you think it matters to me if this company goes out of business tomorrow? We have done the one thing we vowed we would never do—we have hurt our kids. Nothing makes that right. And there's nothing we can do to make it right."

But people would try. He looked at David again. "Has the legal team been notified? Come

Monday morning, people are going to be lining up at courts across the country."

"I have calls in."

"Good. I'm guessing most of the board members have heard, but in case some of them are out of town, I'll call them in the morning." He glanced at his watch. "Later this morning."

Arnie stepped forward. "Jack, I know it's not worth much, but I don't think it was us. Oh, sure, the site crashed, but when we got it back up, it was working fine. The, ah, techs monitoring the site never saw the porn site because it wasn't there. I think there was an override in our server."

Jack stared at him. "You're saying the redirect was external to our system?"

Arnie shrugged. "It's a place to start looking."

The meeting broke up an hour later. After telling everyone to be in by six on Monday morning, Jack sent them home. Samantha stayed on the sofa, not only because she'd come with Jack but because she felt too sick to move.

He collapsed in a club chair and rubbed his temples. "This is completely and totally screwed."

"I feel so horrible," she whispered. "I can't believe this happened. We checked so many times. The security was all there. That's what gets me. The site wasn't compromised. It was the server."

"Regardless of the technicalities, Hanson Media Group is still responsible," he said.

"I know. No one is going to care how it happened, only that it did." She crossed her arms in front of her midsection. "All those children. Who would have done it and why?"

"Not a clue," he admitted. "But I'm going to find out and then that person is going to be prosecuted if I have to do it myself."

Her eyes burned, but she blinked the tears away. Crying wouldn't help anyone. Still, it was hard not to give in to the pain. So many people had worked so hard, only to have everything ruined by someone bent on destroying the company.

"This is revenge," she said. "Or an act of rage. It feels personal."

"To me, too. So who hates me that much and why?"

"Does it have to be someone hating you?" she asked. "Can it be someone who hates the company? A recently fired employee? Someone with a personal grudge against George, or one of your brothers. Who has enemies?"

"Who doesn't?" he asked.

She stared at him. "I'm so sorry, Jack. I thought the new Web site was the answer to all the company's problems. Now I find I've just made things worse."

"You filled all the holes you saw."

"And missed a really big one."

She'd also gotten in the way of his future, she

thought as her stomach clenched tighter. Jack wanted to do his job and get back to his dreams. What were the odds of that happening now? The board was going to be furious and they would blame Jack.

So not fair, she thought frantically. But how could she keep it from happening?

"Jack, I—"

A knock on the door cut her off.

"Come in," he called.

Mrs. Wycliff stepped inside. "The police are here."

Samantha's breath caught. "The police?"

Jack shrugged. "What did you expect?"

Not that. Some of her shock must have shown on her face. He stood and walked toward her.

"It's all right," he said gently. "David is waiting in his office. He'll take you home."

"I don't want you to have to deal with the police by yourself."

He touched her cheek. "Don't worry. You'll

get your chance to answer their questions later today or Monday. Try to get some sleep."

Before she could try to convince him to let her stay, Mrs. Wycliff had ushered her out of the office and into the hallway. There she saw several police officers. They nodded politely.

She walked past them toward David's office. A part of her couldn't believe this was really happening. It was all wrong and there didn't seem to be anything she could do to stop it.

Jack grabbed a couple of hours of sleep Sunday night and was at the office before five on Monday morning. He had multiple crises to deal with.

While it all hit the fan over the Web site disaster, there was still a company to be run. The emergency board meeting started at nine, followed by an afternoon with in-house legal counsel. At last count, there were over a hundred lawsuits ready to be filed as soon as the courts opened. If this didn't kill the company, it would be sheer luck. Best case scenario, Hanson Media Group survived as a smaller, less proud organization which meant cutbacks and massive layoffs.

He was surprised to find Roger waiting outside his office when he arrived.

"Here to confess?" he said, then regretted the words as soon as they were out.

Roger looked at him. "I didn't do it. I'll take a lie detector test if that will help."

Jack looked at the lines of exhaustion on the other man's face, then waved him into the office. "Sorry. I shouldn't have said that. I have no reason to suspect you."

"No more than anyone else with the technical expertise," Roger said bluntly, then handed over a tall cup of Starbucks.

Jack was as startled by the coffee as by Roger's statement. "I was under the impression that you were more a manager than a techie."

Roger sipped his own coffee, then shrugged.

"I'll admit that my first experience with a computer was with punching cards, but I've worked in the business all my life. I might be older and not as fast, but I can code with the best of my team."

News to Jack, as he tried to remember where he'd gotten the idea that Roger didn't know what he was doing on the technical front.

"We've continued to investigate over the weekend," Roger said. "As I suspected from the first, it's not our Web site. The content there never changed and the address wasn't hijacked. Instead, someone got inside the server and messed with it. When the server started to route the user to our site, it made a quick left turn to porn central."

Jack didn't know if the information made a difference or not. "Who did it?"

"I'm still working on that. My guess is someone from this end rather than the server, but the police will be investigating them. I'm in touch with the detective in charge of the case."

"Why do you think it's someone from this company?" Jack asked.

"The attack feels personal. That's just my opinion."

"I appreciate hearing it," Jack told him. "Anything else?"

Roger nodded. "The detective thinks there's a good chance the feds will get involved."

More trouble, Jack thought. No one wanted that. "It's all out of our control," he said. "What are you doing this morning?"

"Continuing the investigation."

"Stay available. I have an emergency board meeting. They may want to ask you more questions."

Roger nodded, then left. Jack stared after him. He'd never liked the man, but suddenly Roger was stepping up to take charge during a crisis. Did he need something like this to show his true nature, or was he the guilty party looking to be close to the action?

Several hours later Jack sat with the board and wished to hell he'd never left his law practice. They were angry and out for blood and right now they didn't particularly care whose.

Baynes, the chairman, led the discussion.

"This has to be fixed, Jack, and the sooner the better."

Jack sat forward and braced his forearms on the table. "I agree, and I'm working on the problem. The in-house IT people are doing what they can to find out who's responsible. I've also hired an outside team to work backwards from the server problem."

"Hired guns?" Baynes asked.

"Independent agents. They don't evaluate what they find, they simply report it. Someone told me this morning that the Web site crash feels personal and I agree with him on that. Someone somewhere wants Hanson Media Group to crash and burn. I want to find out who and I want to know why."

Baynes looked surprised by the information. "A personal attack? Against the company?"

"Until I know who did it, I can't answer that," Jack told him.

"You're working with the police?"

"Yes."

Baynes looked at the papers in front of him. "Samantha Edwards was in charge of the new Web site."

"That's correct. She handled content while coordinating with the IT team on technical aspects."

"According to previous reports, she came up with the whole idea."

Jack saw where they were going and didn't like it. "She had nothing to do with the crash and subsequent rerouting."

"You don't know that for sure," Baynes said.

"Actually, I do. Samantha simply isn't that kind of person and even if she were, she doesn't have the technical expertise."

"She could be working with someone."

"She's not. I know Samantha personally and I'm telling you she's not the one. You're wasting your time with her. She is as devastated as anyone by what happened."

Baynes didn't look convinced, but he changed the subject.

The board broke at noon. Jack barely had an hour until he met with the company's legal counsel. As he hurried into his office, he yelled for Mrs. Wycliff to get Samantha in to see him right away.

He didn't have time for any of this, he thought as he poured coffee and ignored the sandwich his secretary had thoughtfully left on his desk.

Samantha arrived less than five minutes later.

"What's up?" she asked as she walked toward him. "Is it awful? They all have to be furious, but they have to know none of this is your fault."

"They don't know what to think," he told her. "Right now they're looking for information.

They want to talk to everyone involved in the project, including you."

She nodded. "Especially me. I was in charge and it was my idea. I thought this would happen. When do they want to see me?"

"After lunch."

"Okay. No problem. I'll clear my calendar."

She looked tired, but then they all did. It had been a long couple of days. Perhaps anticipating her presence before the board, she'd dressed conservatively—at least for her. A simple blouse over a long, dark skirt. Her hair had been tamed by a clip at the base of her neck.

He led her to the sofa and urged her to sit. He settled next to her.

"They're going to ask a lot of questions," he said. "You don't have very long to prepare. Stay calm and answer as best you can. It would help if you had information to back up your plans."

She frowned. "What kind of information?"

"Your notes. How you came up with the idea of the Web site, the various forms it took. Logs of meetings with your team and the IT people. Transcriptions of discussions."

Samantha stared at him. "You have to be kidding," she said, knowing there was no need to panic, but wanting to all the same. "I don't keep records like that. I barely record the dates and times of our meetings in my date book. Jack, this was a very creative process. We would brainstorm together for a few hours, then go off to work individually. When we got back together, we compared what we had. No one took notes. Sometimes we worked over a game of basketball. You know that."

He nodded. "You'll need to go through the process as logically as you can. Our board members wouldn't be described as creative, so they're not going to understand what you're talking about. They'll want to see your e-mail assigning a task to someone."

"It doesn't exist."

He touched her hand. "It's okay. This is just a conversation. They're going to push you, but that doesn't mean you have to let them. Stand your ground."

She appreciated the advice, but wished she didn't need it. "Are you going to be at the meeting?" she asked.

"I wish I were, but I have to be with legal."

Which made sense, but didn't make her happy. Somehow all this would be easier with Jack in the room.

"I'll be fine," she told him, as much to convince herself. "I have nothing to hide, so what's the worst that can happen? They'll get crabby and I'll endure it. In the meantime I'll go through my notes and see if I can figure out a time line for putting the Web site together. I wonder if Arnie has any information."

"Don't check with him. It will look too much like collusion."

Until that moment, Samantha had only been nervous. Suddenly she was scared. "Jack, do they think it's me?"

"They think it's everyone. The only thing singling you out is that you were in charge. So you've come to their notice. That's all." He squeezed her fingers. "I mean that. I trust you completely."

She saw the sureness in his gaze and allowed herself to draw comfort from it. "You know I would never—"

He cut her off with a quick kiss. "Don't say it. You don't have to. I would suspect myself before you. This isn't about that. It's about an angry board looking for answers. Nothing more."

"Okay." She stood. "I'd better go get ready."

He rose and smiled. "Before you go…"

"What?"

He pulled her close and kissed her. Even as

his mouth brushed against hers, his arms came around her. She leaned against him, savoring the heat and strength of his body.

This was where she belonged, she thought. This was home.

He licked her lower lip and when she parted for him, he slipped his tongue inside. They kissed deeply for a few minutes before they both drew back.

"That could get out of hand in a hot minute," he teased.

"You're right and neither of us have time."

He kissed her lightly. "Rain check."

"We don't even have to wait for bad weather."

"Good to know." He walked her to the door and opened it. "If it gets rough, if they start to get out of hand, excuse yourself and come get me. I mean it, Samantha. Don't let them get to you. They're just regular people."

"Crabby regular people," she told him.

"You'll do fine."

"I'll do my best."

* * *

"Ms. Edwards, what made you come up with the Web site expansion in the first place?"

The woman questioning Samantha was elegant, well-dressed and obviously furious.

"When I heard about the job at Hanson Media Group, I spent several days researching their positioning in the market. I knew cash flow was a problem and that while they needed to grow, another magazine wasn't the answer. The Web site offered a way to expand quickly, and with relatively little start-up capital."

"You've done this sort of thing before? Launched a Web site?" a man asked.

Samantha wished they would all wear name tags, because except for Mr. Baynes, the chairman of the board, she had no clue who anyone was.

"I've been part of a launch," she said. "I've never been completely in charge."

The board members sat on one side of a long table, while she sat on the other. There was a vast expanse of space on either side of her, giving her the sensation of being very, very alone. She knew she could call Jack and he would come defend her, but she wasn't going to take him up on his offer. She would get through this on her own.

"How exactly did you come to work for Hanson Media Group?" Mr. Baynes asked. "You've been hired fairly recently."

"I heard about the job and applied."

"Heard about it how?"

"Helen Hanson told me. We're friends." Samantha clenched her teeth. Should she have admitted to the relationship? She didn't want Helen dragged into this.

"You've known Helen a long time?"

"Over twenty years."

The board members looked at each other.

"Were you jealous of Helen?" the woman

asked. "Did you resent her successful marriage, her personal wealth?"

"What?" Samantha couldn't believe it. "Of course not. What does my relationship with Helen have to do with the Web site?"

"We're looking for a motive, Ms. Edwards."

"I didn't do it," Samantha told them firmly. "I love my job and I'm very supportive of what the company is doing. I would never endanger any child. The team and I worked very hard to make sure we had state-of-the-art security in place. While I do accept responsibility for this happening on my project, I would like to point out that the site itself wasn't compromised. It couldn't have been. Someone got into the server. As that is an outside company and beyond our scope of control, I don't see how we could have prevented that."

"Perhaps if you'd considered the threat," Mr. Baynes said sharply. "Perhaps if you'd looked past your quest for glory."

"My *what?*"

"You were very careful to take the spotlight in all the media interviews, weren't you?"

"No. This is crazy. I was in charge of the project, so it made sense for me to represent the company."

"Something that is normally David Hanson's job," Baynes continued.

Samantha shook her head. "David was with me. We coordinated our activities."

"So you say."

She got it then. She wasn't sure why it had taken so long for her to see the truth. Jack had been wrong—this wasn't an angry board. This was a board looking for a scapegoat. For reasons she couldn't understand, they'd decided that scapegoat was her.

She stood. "However much you search, you are not going to find a motive for me to have sabotaged Hanson Media Group. I wasn't involved in what happened in any way. I don't have a grudge against the company or anyone working for it. I was hired to do a job and I did it to the best of my abilities."

"Hardly a statement to reassure us," the woman said with a sniff.

Samantha ignored her. "I would never endanger any child. That was my mission from the first. To provide them with a safe environment to learn. Every memo, every e-mail, ever letter I've written on the subject supports that."

Baynes narrowed his gaze. "We've spoken with your ex-husband, Ms. Edwards. He describes you as a very emotionally unstable person. After walking out on him for no good reason, you filed for divorce only to change your mind. You begged him to take you back. You threatened his children."

Samantha felt as if she'd been shot. There was a sharp pain in her chest and she couldn't seem to catch her breath. Damn Vance. He'd vowed he would get back at her for leaving him. He'd hated giving up control. By calling Vance, Baynes had handed him a perfect way to get revenge.

"My ex-husband is lying," she said, trying to stay calm. "However, it's very clear to me that you're not going to believe anything I say. What do you want from me?"

"Your resignation," Baynes said.

Right. Then they could issue a press statement and say the person responsible had been punished. The board didn't care about finding the person who had actually done this. They simply wanted to make the news cycle with good news. Something they could toss out in an attempt to salvage the company and the stock price.

"You want me to resign because you don't have any reason to fire me," she said.

"We'll get it soon enough," Baynes told her. "If you go quietly, we won't give the information from your husband to the press."

Talk about a low blow and a threat.

Indecision filled her. Her instinct was to stay and fight, but to what end? Wouldn't her leaving make things easier for Jack? With the board off her back, he could focus on getting the company back on its feet.

She could deal with lies and innuendo, but she didn't want to hurt Jack.

"I'll resign," she said.

Chapter Fourteen

Jack and the legal team took a break close to three. They had already developed a strategy of crisis control and cleanup. Jack did his best to remember his position as president of the company. He knew he was responsible for making sure Hanson Media Group survived. But every time he thought about what had happened, he wanted to throw a chair through the floor-to-ceiling windows.

He left the conference room and headed for

his office to pick up his messages. David fell into step beside him.

"The board is still meeting," his uncle said. "But they've already found one victim."

"That's fast work." He hadn't expected them to act for several weeks. Investigations took time.

"It's Samantha."

Jack didn't break stride. He simply changed directions and headed for the stairs that would take him to the floor where the board met. David stayed with him.

"I know what you're thinking," the older man said.

"I doubt that." Worried, furious, frustrated didn't even come close. Dammit, he'd sent Samantha in there by herself. She'd had to face a firing squad alone and he hadn't been there to protect her.

"Jack, I know you care about her, but think before you act."

"Why? They didn't. How long did they question her? Fifteen minutes? We all know that Samantha isn't guilty of anything. She had great plans for the company. Someone deliberately screwed with that and I'm not going to let him, her or them get away with it."

"What are you going to do?" David asked as they climbed up to the next floor.

"Take control."

He walked into the conference room without knocking. The board was in the middle of questioning several of the IT guys. Jack jerked his head toward the now-open door and the three of them scuttled out.

Jack crossed to the long table, pushed the now-empty chairs aside and leaned toward the seven people who wanted to control his destiny.

"I understand you've had an admission of guilt," he said. "Why didn't you tell me someone had confessed?"

Baynes glared at him. "You're out of line, Jack."

"Not even a little. Come on, Baynes, how are you going to threaten me? Do you want to say you're going to fire me? That would only make my day. So how did you get the confession?"

"Ms. Edwards didn't confess. But as she was ultimately responsible for the program we all thought it was best if she—"

Jack slapped his hands on the table. "*I'm* ultimately responsible. While I'm in charge, then this is my company. You do not have the right to go behind my back and fire my employees for no reason."

"They had a reason," David said, his voice cold. "Tell him, Baynes."

The chairman of the board looked uncomfortable but didn't speak.

"They want to make the news," David said. "They want everyone to think they're making progress so the stock price doesn't tank."

"We care about this company," Baynes said. "Which is more than I can say about either of you."

Jack swore. "I've given everything I had to keep Hanson Media Group from going down. You were all happy about our new program."

"Until there were problems," Baynes said. "Obviously you have incompetent people running things around here. Ms. Edwards has a history of problems and I'm sure they—"

Jack leaned forward and glared at Baynes. "What the hell are you talking about? What problems?"

"We spoke with her ex-husband. He was very forthcoming."

"I'll bet he was."

Jack straightened and took a step back. If he didn't get out of here, he was going to beat the crap out of Baynes and anyone else who stuck around. Samantha must hate him right about now. To think the board had pried into her personal life. He had to find her. He had to know she was all right.

"You want someone to blame," he said. "Blame me. I quit."

Baynes stood. "You can't. We don't accept your resignation. We have a contract, Jack. You violate that and we'll haul you into court. We'll win, too. Then what will happen to your law career?"

Jack started for the old man. David grabbed his arm and pulled him out into the hallway.

"Think," his uncle told him. "Don't make things worse than they are. They're not going to let you go."

"You're right." Jack started for the elevators. "Where's Samantha? Has anyone seen her?"

"Here I am again," Samantha said as she reached for another tissue. "Curled up on your sofa and crying. Isn't this getting boring?"

"Not yet," Helen said with surprising cheer. "You always come for a new and exciting reason. That keeps it interesting."

"Thanks." Samantha knew her friend was trying to keep her from falling too far into the despair pit by using humor but it wasn't exactly working. "I never want to go through anything like that again."

"I don't blame you," Helen said. "I swear, if George leaves the majority shares to me, I'm going to consider firing the board."

Samantha wanted to take that as personal support, but she knew her friend well enough to know that Helen was making a business decision.

"I don't know what to do," she admitted. "I really wanted to stand up to the board, but I don't want to make things worse for Jack. I hate that this is happening to him. Taking over the business was his way of doing the right thing. I know he and his dad weren't close, but when it was important, Jack gave up the job he loved to help out. Now he's getting hit with this. I just wanted to make it better."

"Have you talked to him?" Helen asked.

"No. I sort of lost it and came right here. I guess I should put a call in to him."

Helen smiled. "I have a feeling he'll be looking for you."

"Why?"

"Gee, I don't know. The woman he's been involved with just got bullied by a board of directors he's already annoyed with. Don't you think that will make him react? I won't be surprised to hear he punched out Baynes."

Samantha sat up. "He wouldn't do that."

"Wouldn't he?"

She thought about all the ways Jack had been there for her. How he'd been patient and supportive and more than a little understanding.

"Oh, no," she breathed. "You're right. He's going to be furious." She felt her mouth drop open. "He really cares about me."

Helen rolled her eyes. "You think?"

Samantha grinned. "I care about him, too. I have since we first met."

"That would be the time when you were too scared to hang on to the fabulous guy who was crazy about you?"

"Pretty much." She stood. "What if he thinks this is me running again? What if he doesn't know I'm doing this to help him?"

Helen shrugged. "Have I mentioned how communicating would be a good thing?"

Samantha bent down and kissed her friend's cheek. "You're the best. You know that, right?"

"I've been told before."

Samantha laughed, then grabbed her purse. "I have to go find Jack. If he calls here, would you tell him I'm looking for him?"

Helen reached for the phone. "Just go back to the office. I'll call Mrs. Wycliff so she can let him know you're on your way."

Jack paced in his office, not willing to believe the message until Samantha actually walked in.

"I wasn't leaving," she said as she rushed up

to him. "Well, okay, I was leaving the company, but not you. I thought it would make it easier for you."

"Letting the board pin all this on you?" he asked gruffly, as he pulled her close and stared into her eyes. "Why would having you gone help?"

She smiled. "I had a momentary loss of brain function. It won't happen again."

"Good."

She felt right in his arms. Warm and soft and feminine. Also stubborn, difficult and outrageous and he didn't want her to change a thing.

"Oh, Jack," she said quietly. "This is a really big mess."

"Yeah, but we're going to fix it. For one thing, I've refused to accept your resignation, so don't think you can get out of working here."

"I don't want to try, but I did think of something that may be significant. While I was in the cab from Helen's I wrote out a time line." She pulled a small piece of paper from her purse. "There's something we've all overlooked. The Web site crashed."

He stared at her. "What?"

"Remember? The site went down. The tech guys got it up and running. From this end, the site was fine. But when the site came back online, something happened in the server, switching everyone who logged on to the porn site. I think the two incidents are related. I think the whole thing was rigged to be triggered by the rebooting of the Web site. Which means it could still be an inside job."

He grabbed her shoulders and swore. "It has to be. That's the only thing that makes sense. We've been talking about how this all feels personal. You haven't been around long enough for anyone to hate you—"

"Neither have you," she reminded him.

"I've been around my whole life. Even if I wasn't here, people knew who I was. They knew I wasn't involved. Then my father dies and I come in and take over."

"Or maybe someone was angry at your father and wanted to get back at him through the company."

A real possibility, he thought. He released her and lightly kissed her. "You're pretty smart."

She smiled. "One of my many good qualities. So we have this great theory. Now what?"

"We call in a friend." He walked to the phone and dialed a number. "Roger? It's Jack. Samantha and I have come up with a possible scenario. If I tell you what it is, can you tell me who is capable of doing it?"

He listened carefully, then thanked the man and hung up.

"Well?" Samantha asked. "Are there any names?"

"Two, and one of them is Arnie."

The two men arrived at Jack's office less than ten minutes later. Samantha took one look at them and knew Arnie was the culprit. The truth was there in the way he wouldn't meet her eyes.

Jack invited the two men to sit in the chairs by his desk, but before he could start questioning, she walked up to Arnie.

"Why?" she asked softly. "I thought we were friends. We put in all those late nights together. You had great ideas and I listened. I trusted you. I don't know why you wanted to punish the company and I'll accept that you probably had a good reason, but you hurt children. Innocent children. What about them?"

Arnie stared at her and slowly blinked. "I have no idea what you're talking about."

The man with him, Matt, shifted in his seat. "Me, either. I didn't do it, if that's what you want to find out. The site went down and I worked on that, but I never touched the server." He swallowed. "I have kids of my own. Two. I wouldn't do this."

Samantha never took her gaze off Arnie. "But you would. I thought we were friends."

Jack moved up behind her and put his hand on her arm. "It's not about you, Samantha. It's about me. Am I right, Arnie? It's about me and my father and the company. Because I have it all now. The old man is gone and I have everything."

Arnie sprang to his feet. "You don't deserve it," he yelled. "You don't. You never cared about the business. You never respected your father. Did you think I didn't hear what you said about him? He was a great man. You'll never be like him. Never."

Samantha nearly forgot to breathe. "But you were so supportive of the Web site."

"He was playing you," Jack said tonelessly. "He played us all."

Arnie's lip curled. "You made it so easy. Both of you. I knew your father. We were friends. He liked me. Did you know he talked about you all the time? He missed you and wanted you in his life and you couldn't be bothered. George Hanson was a great man and now he's gone and you don't deserve to run his business. You don't deserve to even sweep the floors."

"So you wanted to take me down," Jack said. "You knew there was a good chance that I would be ruined by the scandal."

Arnie shrugged. "I had high hopes."

Samantha couldn't believe it. "This was your plan from the beginning?"

"Sure thing, babe. Did you really think you were all that?" His expression turned contemptuous. "I had you all fooled. I don't care about what happens to me because the company is ruined. You'll never recover from this. Face it, Jack. You're screwed. You'll stay on to save the sinking ship, but it can't be saved. I made sure of that. The lawsuits will bankrupt you and even before that, no one will ever want to do business with your company again. You're in charge of a worthless empire. And you have me to thank for it."

The door opened and Mrs. Wycliff led in the detective and several uniformed officers. They read Arnie his rights and took him away.

Matt excused himself, as did Mrs. Wycliff, leaving Samantha and Jack alone.

He led her over to the sofa and pulled her down next to him.

"I want to say that was easy," he told her, "but it's just beginning. Knowing Arnie did it and why doesn't clean up the mess any faster."

She snuggled up against him. "At least it gives us a place to start."

He kissed the top of her head. "Maybe I should just give the board what they want. It's going to take years to get the company back on its feet."

She shifted so she could look at him. "Don't you dare. I mean it, Jack. Your dreams are too important to give up. You have a commitment here, so stay for now. But only on your terms.

Don't walk away from everything you've ever wanted just because of this."

"What if what I want is you?" he asked.

Her heart flopped over in her chest. She felt the movement, along with a rush of gladness. Her mouth curved in a smile.

"I would say that's a good thing because I want you, too."

He stared into her eyes. "Seriously?"

"Yes. I've spent so much of my life running from the things that frightened me, but I never once stopped to think about what I might be missing out."

He took her hands in his. "Me, too," he murmured. "I haven't wanted to believe love lasts. For me, it didn't. Now I'm wondering if the reason I couldn't give my heart to someone else is because I'd already given it to you. I love you, Samantha."

Her breath caught. "I love you, too. I think I have from the first moment we met."

"So we wasted ten years?"

"No. We became the people we needed to be to find each other now."

"I like the sound of that."

He pulled her close. She went willingly into his arms. They kissed, their lips clinging.

"We can do this," she told him. "We'll fix Hanson Media Group, then we'll get you back to your law firm. You need to become a judge. You'll look good in black."

He laughed. "Hell of a reason."

She grinned. "Okay. You'll be great at it, too. How's that?"

"I like how you think." He kissed her again. "In fact, I like everything about you."

"I feel the same way about you."

"Want to get married?"

"Yes."

"Just like that? You don't have any questions."

She stared into his eyes. "I love you, Jack. I

trust you and I want to spend my life with you. What questions could I have?"

"I'll do everything I can to make you happy," he told her. "I'll be there for you."

She knew he would. He always had been.

He put his arm around her. "I've been thinking about my brothers. I want to get them to come home. Not just because of the company but because we need to be a family again. You think I could get them back here for a wedding?"

She leaned against him and sighed. "Absolutely. And if they don't agree, we'll hunt them down and drag them back. That could be fun."

He chuckled. "This is why I love you. You always have a plan."

"It's one of my best features."

"And the others?"

"How much I love you."

"Right back at you, Samantha. For always."

* * * * *

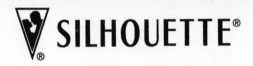

SILHOUETTE®

LARGE PRINT TITLES
DECEMBER 2006 – FEBRUARY 2007

SPECIAL EDITION™

December:	PRODIGAL SON	Susan Mallery
January:	THE BRAVO FAMILY WAY	Christine Rimmer
February:	A MONTANA HOMECOMING ✓	Allison Leigh

December:	WHEN THE LIGHTS GO DOWN	Heidi Betts
January:	CRAVING BEAUTY	Nalini Singh
February:	BABY, I'M YOURS	Catherine Mann

INTRIGUE™

December:	THE LAST LANDRY	Kelsey Roberts
January:	GOING TO EXTREMES	Amanda Stevens
February:	BULLSEYE	Jessica Andersen

Sensation™

December:	FEELS LIKE HOME	Maggie Shayne
January:	THE HEART OF A RULER	Marie Ferrarella
February:	THE PRINCESS'S SECRET SCANDAL	Karen Whiddon

For every kind of woman ❤ *For every kind of mood*

www.silhouette.co.uk